Star of Deltora
THE
HUNGRY ISLE

STAR OF DELTORA

1. Shadows of the Master

2. Two Moons

3. The Towers of Illica

4. The Hungry Isle

THE HUNGRY ISLE

EMILY RODDA

First American Edition 2017
Kane Miller, A Division of EDC Publishing

First published by Omnibus Books a division of
Scholastic Australia Pty Limited in 2016.

Cover type by blacksheep-UK.com
Design and graphics by Ryan Morrison Design.

This edition published under license from Scholastic Australia Pty Limited.

For information contact:
Kane Miller, A Division of EDC Publishing
PO Box 470663
Tulsa, OK 74147-0663
www.kanemiller.com
www.edcpub.com
www.usbornebooksandmore.com

Library of Congress Control Number: 2016934240

Printed and bound in the United States of America

1 2 3 4 5 6 7 8 9 10

ISBN: 978-1-61067-528-4

CONTENTS

1 - Closer

The Isle of Tier was moving, carving a slow, rippling path through the waters of the Silver Sea. Schools of fish dived in panic as the great shadow passed above them, but they were in no danger. The Hungry Isle would not stop to feed today.

Hunched in his cavern, the King of Tier felt the movement thrilling through the magic Staff that stood beside him, its base embedded in his kingdom's earth. For many years he had barely noticed the steady vibration that meant the island was on the prowl. But today he was very aware of it, because today it was accompanied by something new—something that brought beads of cold sweat to his brow.

The Staff had begun tilting a little away from him, towards the sea. It was straining towards a single point in the lonely ocean—a ship that as yet was not even a dot on the horizon.

The King knew why. The ship was the *Star of Deltora*. Aboard was a girl who was bonded to the Staff of Tier by no will of her own, but by the blood that ran in her veins. And the Staff had sensed her.

Britta, breathed the wraiths that twined adoringly about the golden throne, about the hand that held the Staff. *Your daughter, Larsett. Flesh of your flesh. Bone of your bone. She is nearer. Soon she will be with us at last. With us here, with the Staff, forever ...*

Their whispers were eager, thick with longing. Pictures of Britta flickered among them—pictures brought to the cavern by those of their number that had at first been sent to spy on the girl, then had sped back to her with love.

The King could not help but look, though the images made something twist painfully in his chest.

Britta, no longer the child she had been when he last saw her, but a determined young woman who longed to be a trader. Britta creeping from her home while her mother and sister lay sleeping, to compete in the contest that would choose the great Trader Mab's Apprentice and heir. Britta waving farewell to Jantsy the baker's son, whose heart she held in her hand though she did not know it. Britta and her rivals aboard the *Star of Deltora,* making the trading voyage that was to be their final test.

Britta, surrounded by a cloud of adoring wraiths she could not see.

Britta, pretending to be an orphan, fiercely

keeping the dangerous secret that she was the daughter of Dare Larsett, whose name was cursed throughout the nine seas …

The King closed his eyes to shut the pictures out, but still they danced behind his eyelids, tormenting him.

To the last, he had hoped to sense the *Star* leaving Illica, her final trading port, and sailing away to the north, carrying Britta safely home. Instead, the ship had strayed to the southeast, closer to Tier.

Why? By what evil chance—?

Like the stab of a knife it came to him that the wraiths he had sent to bring him news of Britta might be playing their part in drawing the island and the girl together. Bitterness rose in his throat. He tightened his grip on the leaning Staff, and his mind steadied.

The drift of the ship might well have nothing to do with the yearning of the wraiths on board. The weather was not fair for sailing. Only the faintest of breezes stirred the sullen air. The newly risen sun sulked behind a thick blanket of cloud, casting a dull yellow glow over the Silver Sea.

Dimly the King recalled cursing such days in his former life—days when the sails had hung limp above his head and his ship had crept with agonizing slowness through water that seemed as thick as oil.

There had been nothing he could do about the weather then, and there was nothing he could do about it now. With the Staff of Tier at his command he could create wonders from the empty air. He could destroy on the whim of a moment. He could cure all ills. He could live forever.

But for all his might and power, he could not fill the *Star*'s sails and send her far away—any more than he could halt the silent, relentless progress of the island that was drawing nearer to her by the hour.

It was strange to think of it. He had grown used to believing himself all-powerful. Yet slowly he became aware that for some reason he felt more alive now than he had done for many years. It was as if ... as if the present crisis had acted as a tonic, waking him from a long dream.

It came to him that if he dragged the Staff from the island's heart, the island would no longer be able to move, to creep towards Britta. It would cease to be the Hungry Isle, and become as it was when the turtle man Tier first created it from bare rock long ago.

Elation flamed within him, but died almost at once. He knew that he did not have the strength to carry out that plan. The Staff's will was far stronger than his—always had been.

Memories swam up to the surface of his mind. How vivid they were, compared to his vague memories of the trackless time since! Eight years ago, the King thought—eight years or more ... Yet he could see it all as clearly as if it were yesterday.

The reeking chamber in Illica where he knew the pirate Bar-Enoch sprawled dead, the Staff still gripped in a shriveled hand. The triumphant whispering in the dark. The exhausting crawl down the underground stairway with the long, heavy iron box in which the prize lay hidden. The row through the blackness of the night, perilously low in the water, to the anchored *Star of Deltora*. The struggle to load the box into the cargo hold. The feverish, secret celebration.

And then … the growing, nagging call of the Staff from its dark hiding place. The glorious visions of power that at last could not be denied …

And afterward—after the blood and death—standing alone, triumphant, the magic and power of the Staff flowing through his body, flooding his mind. The hazy, black-rimmed island calling to him across the water. The seabirds fluttering down, picking at the dead …

Ah, yes! Throwing the ship's log into the sea. Lowering the landing boat. Drifting slowly into the perfumed haze …

And the wraiths of the island rushing with moaning joy to meet him as he set foot on the glittering black sand and took possession of his kingdom, his destiny, his prison …

Shut in her hot, dim cabin on board the *Star of Deltora*, Britta was thinking of perils far closer at hand than the Hungry Isle. Her eyes kept straying to the mirror that hung above the table where she sat. Her fingers kept brushing aside the bangs that covered her forehead and touching the amber stain that the crew called in dread "the mark of Tier."

"Leave the mark be, Britta, for pity's sake!" hissed Jewel of Broome, jumping from her bunk and beginning to pace the cabin restlessly. "It is not going to disappear from one minute to the next!"

Britta looked up at the tall figure of her friend. Jewel's brows were knitted, and her skin was shining with sweat. Even her shaved head gleamed.

"Go on deck, Jewel, and get some air!" Britta urged. "I have to hide myself away from the crew but you do not, and I know you feel stifled in here. I am perfectly safe alone—during the day, at least. And Vashti is in her cabin, I think, just a few steps away."

"Surely you do not believe that Vashti would help you!" Jewel growled. "That girl would not lift a finger to help a rival—or anyone else, come to think about it." She stopped by the porthole, twitched the curtain aside and stared out.

Britta sighed. "If only Mab were not ill! She would soon make the men see reason. But surely, before too long, they will realize for themselves that Captain Hara is right and they have nothing to fear from me."

Jewel turned from the porthole. Her brown face looked strangely bleached. She seemed about to speak, but before she could say anything there was a tap on the cabin door. The door opened a little, and a cropped gray head appeared in the gap.

"Healer Kay!" Britta exclaimed.

Kay slipped into the cabin, closing the door behind her. Her worried eyes searched Britta's face then slid quickly away again to glance at Jewel.

Britta felt a stab of fear. "Is Mab worse?" she heard herself ask.

"No worse—though very weak and feverish." Kay dropped into the chair opposite Britta, wearily leaning her elbows on the table. Her face, usually so calm, looked strained.

"I—I hope you both understand that my first loyalty must be with Mab," she said abruptly.

"Of course," said Britta, staring at her in confusion. "You are her healer."

"Yes. And have been so for seven years—ever since the day I was called to tend to her for a poisoned finger in Dorne, where I lived then." Kay's lips twisted into a rueful smile. "The old crab had fallen out with every healer she had ever had before me, but somehow I took to her and she to me. I have sailed with her ever since. For all her faults, I must stand by her."

She darted a sideways glance at Britta. Britta thought of the precious sunrise pearl that Mab had forced her to give up as their price for leaving Illica, then let the bitter memory slide away.

"I understand, Kay," she managed to say.

"It is the same story with Hara," Kay went on, as if she had not heard. "After Captain Mikah left Mab's service to sail with Dare Larsett—a mistake that led him to his death—Mab could not find another captain to suit her. But five years ago she met Hara. She lured him away from his home port in the Ocean of the South, and now I truly believe he would lay down his life for her."

"I am sure," Britta murmured, trying to ignore the clamor that her father's name always raised in her mind. With a chill, it came to her that perhaps she was being warned not to expect Kay or Hara to protect her from the crew, if protecting her would do Mab harm.

The same idea had obviously occurred to Jewel.

"I am here for Britta," she said. "And so is Sky of Rithmere." Her voice sounded harsh and strange to Britta's ears. It was almost as if Jewel was afraid.

"I know that," Kay said, "and I am glad of it. The men are in an ugly mood. According to Sky, none of them believes Mab's tale that you stole that sunrise pearl, Britta. They all think you found it in Two Moons, by sorcery. Bosun Crow is doing nothing to calm them—quite the reverse, I fear."

She sighed. "It seems they have begun to talk of the *Star*'s evil history again, too. It is as if the horror of the ship's first voyage with Dare Larsett counts for more than all the voyages she has made since, under the Rosalyn flag. These men are all new to the *Star*—that is the trouble! Our regular crew would never—"

"If that troublemaker Crow is still going about saying I am a witch, and a curse on the ship, it is *he* who should be kept below!" Britta burst out angrily.

"I fear Crow is not the only one saying it now." Kay looked at Jewel, who was still standing by the porthole, the corner of the curtain gripped in her hand. "Have you seen?" she asked abruptly.

Jewel nodded. Silently she beckoned to Britta, and pulled the curtain back.

"What is it?" Britta cried, very irritated. "I know the wind has not freshened, Jewel! I can feel that as well as you can!"

Jewel simply pulled the curtain farther. Her eyes were very dark and her skin looked almost gray. Britta's heart seemed to leap into her throat.

She hurried to the porthole and looked out. The sky was filmed with cloud through which the sun glowed sullenly, casting an eerie yellow light. The sea was dull and oily looking. At first she could see nothing unusual. And then she began to pick out dark shapes beneath the surface of the water, many, many dark shapes, and as she realized what they were, the hair on the back of her neck began to prickle.

"Turtles!" she whispered.

"They are following the ship," said Kay. "They are all around us. They came from nowhere—hundreds of them. And more every minute."

2 - Ship of Fear

For the rest of that day, and for two days after that, Britta stayed out of sight, battling a mounting sense of dread. The turtles swarming around the ship had made the mark on her brow seem even more like the sign of a foul disease.

Davvie, the ship's boy, brought her meals. Sky had made a single hurried visit and left after saying very little. Vashti, of course, kept well away. The only sign of her presence on the *Star* was the soft opening and closing of her cabin door.

Jewel came in and out, looking increasingly troubled and bringing news that grew worse by the day. Mab was still unwell. Captain Hara was barely sleeping, manning the wheel all night and snatching catnaps through the day. He had thundered at Crow because Crow kept insisting that the ship was straying off course and that the mass of turtles was to blame.

The crew was very tense. There had been several fights. A man called Wrack had been gravely injured after falling from the rigging. And there were tales of groans and ghostly wails in the night.

"The only person on board who looks happy is Vashti," Jewel said. "She is cock-a-hoop. She thinks that I am disqualified for my trouble in Illica and that you will have nothing to show the Trust Committee, so the prize is hers. That is all she cares about. The girl is a fool, as well as a cheat. She seems to have no idea what is happening on this ship."

Britta nodded listlessly, turning the hair clip she had found in Bar-Enoch's cavern over and over in her fingers so that the rare blue odi shells winked in the dim light.

Perhaps the clip would win the contest for her—perhaps it would not. At this moment it was hard to think about the future—or even to care about it very much. Imagining her life after the voyage was like trying to see through a thick, ominous mist. She felt a dull ache at the thought of losing the *Star of Deltora*, but that was all.

Jewel never spoke about mutterings of witchcraft, and Britta did not ask. There was no need. The way Davvie scratched timidly at the cabin door, thrust the tray into her hands and scurried away looking fearfully over his shoulder, told her more than she wanted to know.

She found herself smoothing her hair over her

brow again and again, even when, as so often, she was quite alone. She felt jittery and sick. The sticky air of the cabin seemed to jump with shadows and seethe with whispers.

She could not concentrate on the books Jewel brought her from the reading room. And as for her old friend, *A Trader's Life*—she was afraid to open its tattered covers. She knew that if she did, she would be compelled to turn to the tale called "The Wondrous Staff of Tier," and read of the turtles that had swarmed to the sorcerer Tier's aid after his enemies on Two Moons had cast him adrift.

In the end, she spent long hours simply lying on her bunk, with the little clay manikin she had brought from Two Moons perched on the pillow beside her. The goozli was company of a kind, and seemed to hold the shadows back.

She kept being drawn to the porthole. Over and over again she looked out, hoping that the scene had changed. But it was always the same. The muffled sun still cast its unearthly light. The leaden sea was still thick with swimming turtles.

Late on the third afternoon, sick at heart, she closed the porthole curtain and sat down at the writing table. Delighted to have something to do, the goozli sprang onto the tabletop and busily began to fold the dingy white shirt that it had mended for her that morning.

"I cannot go on like this, goozli," Britta

murmured. "What in the nine seas am I to do?"

The goozli dropped the shirt and gazed at her mournfully, its small mouth turned down. It looked around as if trying to think of something that might cheer her, and abruptly pounced on the odi shell hair clip. Scampering up Britta's arm, it gathered up a few locks of hair from each side of her face, deftly lifted them onto the top of her head, and used the clip to fasten them in place.

Britta looked in the mirror. Even in her misery, she could see that the new style suited her. The tiny shells on the clip gleamed like blue jewels against the darkness of her hair. Standing on her shoulder, the goozli put its hands on its hips and nodded with satisfaction. She could not help smiling.

"Thank you, goozli," she murmured. "That looks very nice."

And then, very suddenly, it came to her on a wave of fear that if anyone should see her now, see her talking to a little clay figure that could move and think and do her bidding, that person would be certain that she was a witch indeed.

And perhaps … perhaps in a twisted sort of way that person would be right—if to be a witch was to have magic at your command.

Britta pressed her sweating hands together. Her heart was thudding hard in her chest. She had become so used to the goozli that she had started to take it for granted. She had certainly stopped wondering at the power of the magic that had created it. There had been so much else to think about!

But now, as the goozli jumped nimbly from her shoulder and began pottering about the writing table, tidying the books and pencils scattered there, Britta looked at it with new eyes. And the more she looked, the more her fear grew.

The little creature was so small, so charming and eager to please! It had been easy for Britta to forget that it could be far more powerful than she knew.

But the goozli had been shaped from the rare amber mud in the heart of the Two Moons swamplands. It had been made by Thurl, leader of the strange tribe called the turtle people and heir to the ancient magic of the sorcerer Tier.

Were turtles swarming now around the *Star of Deltora* because the goozli was aboard? If so … Britta glanced at the curtained porthole. If so, there was a simple answer to the problem. Wait till night. Open the porthole. Throw the little clay figure into the sea. It would make only the tiniest splash. And perhaps, when she looked out of the porthole in the morning, the turtles would be gone.

As if the goozli had felt her thoughts, it turned to look at her. Its tiny eyes were dull. Its mouth seemed to tremble.

Yet somehow Britta knew that whatever she decided, the goozli would accept its fate. Before it had dried, when it was still soft and new, her fingertips had marked it, just as its clay had marked her brow with a stain that nothing would clean away. Bonded to her from its beginning, the goozli was hers to do with as she wished. She could treasure it or she could destroy it. Its destiny was in her hands.

And for that very reason, she knew she could not do what cold common sense urged her to do. She could not sacrifice the goozli—especially on a theory that might not even be true.

"You are mine and I am yours," she said to the little creature gazing up at her. "We belong together, and together we will stay, whatever comes of it."

That night, Jewel came in from dinner looking grave. "Wrack died at sunset," she said. "Kay did her best for him, but it was no use."

She knelt by her bunk and pulled her storage drawer out as far as it would go. She felt in the space behind it and drew out the knife and the leather pouch of spears that had been hidden there since the voyage began. Britta's throat closed.

"I swore to Mab that I would not go armed on the ship," Jewel remarked, calmly testing the point of each spear with her thumb. "Still, I think she will forgive me for breaking my oath as things are at present."

"Jewel—" Britta faltered.

"Trouble is ahead, Britta. I feel it, Sky feels it, Kay feels it and so does Hara, though he pretends otherwise.

Vashti seems to feel nothing, but then Vashti lives in a little bubble of her own. As far as she is concerned, the men are just parts of the ship, no more human than the planks beneath her feet. She cannot imagine their being any danger to her."

"And—Mab?"

Jewel took a cloth from the drawer and began wiping dust from the spear shafts, one by one. "According to Kay, Mab will be on deck at dawn for Wrack's funeral, though she is still very weak. Mab says it is her duty, and feels her presence may calm the crew. Perhaps it will—we can only hope."

"I am the one the men fear," Britta found herself saying. "This is all my fault."

Jewel swung round and grinned at her. "I wondered when that was coming. Sky and I had a wager on it, in fact, and he won because you did not say it yesterday. Will you offer to throw yourself into the sea now, to save us all?"

"No," Britta admitted, half angry, half laughing.

"Then stop talking of fault. As Hara says, only an ignorant fool would believe that you could attract turtles to the ship or make us veer off course in the night. But Crow *is* an ignorant fool, and sadly he is also a bully who has the weaker men under his thumb."

Britta sighed. "It all began when the Keeper of Maris claimed to sense a fearful presence aboard the *Star*, and would not allow us to land. Even you were afraid then, Jewel."

A shadow passed over Jewel's face. "I am still afraid. But I do not blame any person. I blame the ship."

"No!" cried Britta in dismay. "The *Star*—"

"Whatever Kay says, the *Star of Deltora* may be cursed," Jewel said soberly. "The rumor is that she has never been refitted. Except for the landing boat, which was missing and had to be replaced, this ship is the same, in every detail, as she was when Dare Larsett killed her first crew and set her adrift."

"Yes," Britta whispered, "but—"

"And now Sky tells me that a metal box that once held the cursed Staff of Tier still lies in the cargo hold!" Jewel bared her teeth. "Who knows what phantoms cling to it? I do not wonder the men have been hearing ghostly wails in the night!"

Remembering what she had felt in the hold, what she had heard and seen looking down at the iron box, Britta could not answer.

Memories, she told herself. Only memories trapped in the ship's timbers, like the memories in the stone of Bar-Enoch's cavern. But somehow she was no longer so sure.

"It is not phantoms we have to fear at present, however." Jewel turned back to her work, pushing a clean spear back into the pouch and selecting another. "Best you stay dressed tonight, Britta, in case of trouble. But rest easy. Sky is on the alert, and no one will get to you while I am here."

No doubt Jewel meant well, but nothing she could have said would have been more likely to rob Britta of sleep. Having climbed to her bunk, pausing only to shed her boots, she lay awake hour after hour, jumping at every sound.

She thought of the man Wrack, his body no doubt already sewn into a canvas shroud, waiting for the dawn when it would be given to the sea that had been his life.

She thought of Healer Kay, watching over Mab, and Captain Hara standing grimly at the wheel, guiding the ship through the sullen night.

She even thought of Collin and Vorn, the Illican runaways whose escape had caused her present trouble. By now their tiny, doomed craft would be lost in a wilderness of sea. She imagined them clinging together, asleep beneath the blanket of cloud, snatching a few moments of forgetfulness.

In the early hours of the morning her thoughts drifted to Jantsy, to Captain Gripp, who had put her name down for the Rosalyn contest, to her sister, Margareth, and her mother, Maarie. But the images of these people—the loved, familiar faces, symbols of home—were vague and shadowy. The city of Del seemed like another world, like a place she had once seen in a dream. Reality was this dark, stifling cabin where she lay in dread, listening to Jewel's quiet breathing and waiting for an angry pounding on the door.

3 - The Demand

As feeble light began filtering through the porthole curtain, as she heard Jewel sigh and swing her legs to the floor, Britta knew that her long watch had been for nothing. The night had passed without alarm. Wearily she closed her eyes and fell into a light doze. She half heard Jewel moving quietly about, and after a while the door opened and clicked shut.

She has gone to Wrack's funeral, Britta thought. Everyone will be present, except me. But no one would want me there in any case—Wrack least of all.

She was too tired for the thought to give her pain. She turned her head on the pillow and drifted back to sleep.

This time her sleep was deep. She did not stir as light slowly strengthened behind the porthole curtain. Dreams eddied through her sleeping mind, one dream merging into another. She was in Del, in the hidden cellar of the potter Sheevers, whose treasures were packed in a long metal box. She was on the isle of the Keeper in Maris, trying to read some misty words on a smooth rock wall …

And then she was behind the counter at home, in the little shop in Del. She was telling her mother that she had brought home a surprise. She was dipping her fingers into her apron pocket and pouring a handful of sunrise pearls into the cash box. But instead of smiling, Maarie began to scream in horror, and Britta realized that what she had thought was a counter was the shell of a vast turtle.

The turtle raised its head and stared at the mark on her brow with unblinking amber eyes. The cash box slid to the floor and the precious pearls spilled out, rolling under the door into the street, dropping through gaping cracks between the floorboards. And still Maarie screamed and screamed …

Britta woke in terror, her heart racing. She lay panting, her mother's last scream still echoing in her mind. It was only a dream, she told herself furiously. A stupid dream …

Then the scream came again—high, piercing—not in her mind, but from somewhere above her head.

She threw herself out of her bunk, half sliding down the narrow ladder. The memory of her nightmare still clung to her, but now she knew that the screams her mind had woven into the dream's fabric had been real. They were what had woken her.

It was Vashti who had screamed, Britta was sure of it. Mab would not scream like that, nor Healer Kay, nor Jewel. What had happened to make Vashti lose her perfect control so completely?

Shadows flickered in the corners of Britta's eyes as she thrust her feet into her boots and blundered out of the cabin. In the corridor she stopped, listening. The screams had stopped, but a rumble of voices drifted down the steps that led up to the main deck.

"Drop your weapons!" someone bawled suddenly. "Drop them, or his death will be on your head!"

There was a heavy clatter, then the sound of thudding footsteps.

Britta stole to the stairway and began creeping up. She had taken only two steps when she froze. Someone was standing by the head of the stairs, framed against the weird yellow glare of the clouded sun. Slowly Britta made out a pair of tall boots and brown legs bound with strips of leather ...

Jewel.

Britta breathed out, and took another step. The legs shifted, very slightly, and she knew that Jewel had heard her. Jewel's hand appeared, holding a crumpled ball of paper. The long fingers relaxed, and the ball of paper dropped onto the top step and rolled down to the next.

Britta reached for it and flattened it out. As she read the words scrawled upon it, a red mist began to gather before her eyes.

Captain Hara —

We accuse the female Britta of witchcraft. Here are some of the many proofs of her sorcery.

* She can see through walls and see in the dark. This is proved by the way she flits around the ship as if she has known it all her life, though this is her first voyage.
* She is in league with the Two Moons turtle people, who worship the sorcerer Tier. This is proved by the mark of Tier on her brow. Also by the fact that she found a sunrise pearl.
* She cast a spell on a man of Illica to make him abandon his bride on the eve of his wedding, and go to a certain death.
* Since Trader Mab angered her by forcing her to give up the sunrise pearl, she has caused Mab to sicken.
* She caused a tempest that nearly sank the ship, and saved herself by magic when she fell overboard.
* She has raised spirits in the belly of the ship to howl in the night.
* She has caused the wind to fail and called the turtles of the sea to steer the ship off course.
* She caused the death of our crewmate, Wrack.

She is the evil the Keeper of Maris felt. She threatens us all. We demand that she be set adrift and left to her fate. If our demand is not met, we will be forced to take matters into our own hands.

Her mouth dry, Britta let the paper fall. The goozli stirred in her pocket as if it could feel her terror. Shadows twined feverishly around her, but for once she was able to ignore them, for what was there to fear in echoes of the past, compared to the dread reality of the present?

"Did you get it all, Bolt?" she heard Crow's voice bawl.

"Aye," Bolt shouted back. "Spears an' knife, both."

"Right, Jewel, or whatever your unnatural name is," Crow sneered. "Fetch the witch up an' be quick about it."

Jewel's body tensed, but she did not move.

"Do it, you witch-loving savage!" Crow bellowed. "You know what'll happen if you don't!"

It was enough. Britta stumbled to the top of the steps. She forced her way past Jewel and turned to the crowded stern.

The first person she saw clearly was Vashti, cringing by the rail, her hands pressed to her mouth. The second person was Mab, looking like death. And the third was Captain Hara, standing as still as a statue, with Crow's knife at his throat.

Crow was sweating. His bloodshot eyes were hot with a strange, fearful excitement. When he saw Britta, he bared his teeth like an animal.

"So, you've decided to show yourself," he growled. "Well, don't try any of your sly witch's tricks on me! The Captain's dead if you do, an' every hand here'll bear witness that it was no fault of mine."

"This is mutiny, Crow!" Hara growled. "I warn you—"

"You warn *me?*" Crow almost squealed, pressing the knife closer so that Hara's head was forced back to avoid the point of the blade. "No, I warn *you*, Captain! I warn you to stay still an' keep your gob shut. I'm master on this ship now, an' you've only got yourself to blame. Isn't that right, men?"

A rumble of agreement rose from the crew ranged behind him, though some men looked frightened or ashamed as they spoke, and a few, like Grubb the ship's cook, did not open their lips at all. Little Davvie, crouching to one side with the cat Black Jack clutched in his arms, was plainly terrified.

Britta searched for Sky and suddenly caught sight of him lounging against the mast a little behind Davvie. Sky looked perfectly relaxed, but she knew him too well by now to be deceived. He met her eyes, his long fingers playing absently with one of the charms tied in his braided hair.

As if it was the most important thing in the world, Britta strained to see if the charm was the little boat that was supposed to ensure safety at sea or the dagger that gave protection from enemies.

"All you had to do was bow to our fair an' just demand, Captain," Crow went on in a hectoring tone. "It was fair an' just, wrote down on paper as is proper, an' to which all hands agreed, being in dread fear of our lives. An' what did you do but screw up what we wrote an' chuck it away like it was a piece of rubbish!"

The knife jerked in his hand and the point pierced Hara's skin. Hara made no sound as a thin rivulet of blood began trickling down his straining neck to pool on the white collar of his shirt.

"Bolt!" Crow roared. "Lower the landing boat! These Rosalyn witch lovers an' their fancy are going over the side—the whole lot of them."

"No!" Vashti screamed, as Bolt and a few other men scuttled to obey the order. "No, no, no!"

There was only one thing to be done. Britta could see that as plainly as she could see the blood staining Hara's shirt, the deathly pallor of Mab's skin and the superstitious dread on the faces of the crew.

"Your quarrel is with me, Crow," Britta heard herself saying. "Do what you like with me—I will not try to stop you—but let the others be. They are not to blame for trying to defend me. They have nothing to do with this."

She heard Jewel mutter her name. She saw Sky slowly push himself away from the mast.

"You heard her!" Vashti cried wildly to Crow. "Do as she says! She is nothing to us! Spare me and my parents will reward you richly, I swear it!"

"Might be best, Crow," mumbled Grubb. "Getting rid of the witch is one thing—like you say, no one can blame us for that. Getting rid of the others ..."

He shrugged uneasily.

Crow scowled. "No," he spat. "I don't trust them. With them aboard, ten to one I'll wake up one night with a blade in my guts. Besides ..." He ran his thick tongue over his bottom lip and his bloodshot eyes glittered. "Besides, with this lot gone, the ship's ours—ours for good."

"Crow, you cannot do this!" Healer Kay cried. "Mab is ill! It is murder!"

"Button your lip, Healer!" Crow spat. "You can't scare me with talk of murder. Putting you off in a seaworthy boat isn't the same as killing, so long as we give you food an' water. As for the old woman—well, she'll be serpent bait soon whether she stays or goes. She's been ailing since we left Del harbor—anyone with half an eye could see that!"

He gave a violent start as Mab raised her head and stood upright, pushing away Kay's hand.

"Your note to Captain Hara claimed that Britta was killing me by witchcraft, Bosun," Mab said, in a warm, amused voice that was in startling contrast to her haggard looks. "Now you are saying that I have been dying all along. Which is it to be? You cannot have it both ways, you know."

4 - Black Jack

A few of the men ranged behind Crow chuckled uneasily. Recovering from his shock, Crow hunched his shoulders and glowered at Mab. "Who are you to tell me what I can have an' what I can't, old woman?" he blustered.

"I am the Trader Rosalyn, the owner of this ship," Mab said, with a slight smile. "I am the one who offered double pay to all members of the crew who remain loyal until we dock in Del. And I am the one who will see to it that this promise is kept, if I am allowed to reach Del myself. Despite what you say, Bosun, I am not quite ready to feed the serpents yet."

Again there were chuckles from the men, and a few admiring guffaws as well. Hope fluttered in Britta's chest.

Crow's mouth twitched, and a nerve began jumping beneath his left eye.

"You are putting yourself and the other men in the wrong for no good reason, Crow," Mab went on, letting her gaze wander to the faces of the crew. "I quite understand how you have come to feel the way you do, but you are mistaken. In fact, the only danger you face is the danger of becoming outlaws, hunted through the nine seas for the rest of your lives."

She was magnificent! The only sign of what the performance must be costing her showed not in her face but in Healer Kay's tight mouth and Kay's arm, tensed to catch her if she fell.

But Mab did not fall, nor did she falter.

Behind Crow's back, the men were gazing at her as if hypnotized. And as for Hara … sweat was rolling down the Captain's brow, but his eyes, fixed on Mab, glowed with naked devotion.

Crow licked his lips. "The witch—" he began in a high voice.

"Britta is no more a witch than I am, man," Mab said, with a touch of amused contempt. "She is merely a clever little minx who can persuade people to do things she wants them to do, and will steal when she can. I daresay she has been creeping about the ship by night, prying into its secrets and causing some of the noises that have robbed you of sleep and made you prey to accidents. But all that is over now."

The scathing words washed over Britta without touching her. She knew that Mab was fighting for all their lives in the only way she could. And Mab was winning. The men had begun glancing at one another. Many had begun casting dubious looks at Crow.

"I cannot promise that we will have plain sailing ahead," Mab added, gazing steadily at the crew. "No voyage is without its dangers, as you men know only too well. But I can assure you, at least, that no trouble we may face from now on will be young Britta's doing."

She smiled slightly, as if she was sure that the men must now agree that the very idea of such a thing was ridiculous. The shamefaced smirks in her audience seemed to show that she was right. It did not seem to matter that she had not even tried to answer most of the charges against Britta. Her mellow, confident voice, ringing with authority, had triumphed where a hundred logical arguments might have failed.

"Here is my proposal," Mab continued. "If you now release Captain Hara and return to your duties, the offer of double pay still stands. In addition, this matter will not be raised again between us, nor will it be reported in Del. Every one of you will leave the *Star of Deltora* without a stain on his character."

There was a rumble of sound from the men—a low, relieved sound. Crow showed the whites of his eyes.

"Well?" said Mab. "Is it a bargain?"

And at that moment, just when it seemed that her success was assured, fate took a hand. Perhaps Davvie, in his fear and tension, had squeezed Black Jack a little too tightly. Perhaps the cat simply grew tired of being held. Whatever the reason, the result was disastrous.

Black Jack struggled violently, broke free from Davvie's grip, shook himself indignantly and stalked away from the mast with his tail held high. He was making for the prow, no doubt in search of peace and solitude, when he came face-to-face with Britta, and saw what no one else could see. He saw the wraiths of Tier, curling about the girl like smoke.

Instantly he stopped dead, his claws digging into the boards of the deck. His fur stood on end, his back arched and he hissed, his eyes blazing.

"You see?" Crow howled. "The creature knows! It knows what she is!"

The men groaned and cursed in terror. Britta did not hear them. She stood frozen in a whirlwind of whispers, staring in shock at Black Jack's wild, golden eyes, his gaping pink mouth, his bared white teeth. A memory was twitching at the edge of her mind. It was the key to the horror—somehow she knew that—but the more she tried to drag it into the light, the more it danced out of her reach.

With a yowl the cat spun round and streaked away through the legs of the shocked, staring men.

"What more proof do you need?" Crow yelled. "Do we all have to die before you stir your miserable carcasses an' do what no soul in the nine seas would blame you for doing? Get the witch an' all who tried to save her off this ship! Get them off!"

A wave of panicking men overwhelmed the

small group standing by the rail. Vashti screamed and screamed again as rough hands were laid upon her. Mab staggered and sagged back into Kay's arms.

Britta felt Jewel's grip on her arm break as the woman of Broome, cursing and struggling, was dragged back by Bolt and the others who had helped launch the landing boat.

"The Rithmere sneak as well!" Crow shouted. "He's one of them!"

"No!" Davvie cried shrilly, as two men seized Sky and began dragging him away. "Not Sky! Sky hasn't done nothing!"

"Keep quiet, boy, or you'll find yourself over the side with him!" Crow snarled. He raised his voice. "An' that goes for anyone else who don't like what I'm saying. Any man wants to object, now's his chance. Well? Speak up!"

No one said a word. Cowed and sweating, Grubb hung his head. His neighbors shuffled their feet, their eyes troubled but their mouths shut tight.

Crow grinned. Holding his knife steady, he snatched the captain's cap from Hara's head and clapped it on his own.

"All right, scum!" he growled. "Move!"

The end came quickly after that. In very few minutes, it seemed, Britta was crawling across the benches of the landing boat, removing herself as far as possible from Sky, Jewel and Vashti, who had followed her over the side of the ship. She sank onto the short, narrow seat in the boat's prow and crouched there, numb with shock. Shadows were swarming around her. Soft, echoing voices whispered her father's name.

The landing boat must be as drenched in memories as the ship itself, Britta thought vaguely. There seemed something odd or wrong about this, but she could not think what, and soon stopped trying.

Jeering faces stared down over the ship's rail as Mab, swinging at the end of a rope like a bundle of rags, was lowered into Jewel's arms. Pale with outrage, Healer Kay scrambled down next. And last of all came Hara, his face set like stone.

"Take the oars," Hara muttered to Sky and Jewel, jerking his head at the rowing bench in the boat's center. "Get us well clear as soon as they cast off. I would not put it past Crow to try to run us down."

Silently Sky and Jewel obeyed, leaving Kay to make Mab as comfortable as she could.

Huddled in the prow, locked in a whispering nightmare, Britta heard Crow's voice bellowing orders in the ship above. She heard the heavy splash as a rope was cast off carelessly, and a few raucous cheers as the landing boat floated free. She saw Hara heave the dripping rope on board. She saw Jewel and Sky bend to the oars. She roused herself a little, forcing the whispers back.

"How is she?" Hara muttered, looking down at Mab's gaunt face.

"Bad," said Kay tightly. "That performance with

Crow cost her dearly. A week drifting in an open boat will finish her."

Hara set his jaw. "It will not be so long, and we will not be drifting. We will be rowing—as hard and fast as we can. I have my compass. The map of the Silver Sea is in my head. I know where we are, and I know which way to go. Be assured, Kay, I will not fail Mab now."

"Indeed?" Kay murmured, giving him a strange look. "And what of the rest of us?"

"Speaking for myself, I will be more than happy to return to Illica, whatever anyone else might think!" Vashti declared in a high voice, with an angry glance at Britta.

Staring dully back at her, Britta felt a faint stab of pity. How could Vashti think that Hara meant to make for Illica? Illica was far behind them now, and Mab would not survive a long, hard journey. Hara's loyalty was to Mab, and only Mab. His plan must surely be to find land—any land—as quickly as possible.

Britta waited for the captain to tell Vashti so, but he said nothing. No doubt he was wise. Vashti would find out her mistake soon enough, and why condemn everyone to her fury before then? Vashti had not been brought up to hardship, and the idea of landing on a tiny dot in the ocean for Mab's sake would fill her with rage and terror.

White sails swelled high above them and the *Star of Deltora* began to move. The landing boat bobbed a little in the wash, but by now was too far from the ship to be in danger.

I have lost the *Star*, Britta thought, as the gap between the ship and the boat widened. I have lost her again—this time, forever.

A memory floated into her mind—her father saying that he had named the ship *Star of Deltora* because for lost travelers stars were beacons in the darkness, guides to be trusted. And slowly it came to her that the *Star of Deltora* had indeed been like a flaming beacon in her life. The beautiful ship had been at the heart of her longing for the life she had lost when her father failed her.

She had loved and trusted the *Star* as once she had loved and trusted Dare Larsett. She had followed her love blindly, from that moment in Captain Gripp's cottage when she had agreed to enter the Trader Rosalyn contest. And every step she had taken since had brought her closer to this—this small, creaking boat, this sullen waste of sea.

The mutineers had begun cheering once more, and this time the sound drifting back from the ship was deeper, stronger and more heartfelt. It sounded as if every hand aboard was rejoicing.

Without surprise, Britta saw the reason. The *Star of Deltora* was surging through clear water. The turtles that had surrounded the ship for so many days had fallen behind. They were letting the ship go, and massing instead around the landing boat.

5 - The Turtle Tide

Jewel cursed in shock as her oar was almost torn from her hands, its blade jammed between the huge, humped creatures suddenly swarming in the water beside her. At the same moment, Sky jerked back, nearly falling from his seat as his oar too was fouled.

"Ship the oars!" Hara bellowed as the boat rocked violently and water poured over the sides. "Don't lose them, for pity's sake!"

His shouts were almost drowned out by everyone else's cries of alarm, but it did not matter. Jewel and Sky had both grown up with boats, and knew what had to be done. Already they were skillfully freeing their oars and dragging them in to safety.

In moments they had succeeded, without damage or loss. Water lapped around their ankles as they slumped forward, panting, on the rowing bench.

Hara surveyed the great, dark circle of swimming

turtles that surrounded the boat on all sides. Then he turned to look at Kay, sitting expressionless in the stern with Mab's head resting on her shoulder.

"We are not to be allowed to row, it seems," the healer said quietly.

His lips a thin, hard line, his hair and beard draggled with spray, Hara reached for the bucket under his bench and doggedly began to scoop water from the bottom of the boat.

"This is your fault!" Vashti shrieked at Britta through chattering teeth. "You and your sunrise pearl! You stole it from the turtle people to win the contest, and now they have sent their creatures after you, in revenge! You have killed us all!"

"We are not dead yet, Vashti," drawled Sky. "And, by the by, if you really believe that these turtles followed us, invisible, all the way south from Two Moons, you are as stupid as Crow."

As Vashti glared at him, speechless with outrage, he shrugged. "The turtles gathered around the ship just out of Illica. Does it not seem likely, then, that they live in *this* part of the Silver Sea, and have nothing to do with Two Moons, or sunrise pearls, at all?"

"So this may not be quite the disaster it seems," Jewel put in stoutly. "Turtles breathe air, and these turtles have been swimming for days. They will surely want to return to their home island soon, so they can rest. If they carry us along with them, we may find ourselves on land very soon."

"Indeed we may," Kay murmured. "As in the old tale."

Hara hesitated, then nodded and returned to his baling. Sky said something under his breath and began fingering one of the charms threaded in his hair.

Britta slid farther back on her bench and stared down at her hands. A great, aching lump had risen in her throat. After the terrible scene with Black Jack, she had fully expected to be treated as an outcast by everyone aboard the landing boat. Yet Kay and Hara, despite their fears for Mab, had not uttered a word against her. And Sky and Jewel had defended her as if she deserved it, and as if they still thought of her as a friend.

But I do not deserve it, Britta thought, the pain in her throat becoming as sharp as a knife thrust. The mark of the turtle man Tier on my forehead is plain for everyone to see. But no one in this boat knows about the goozli. No one knows that I carry the living magic of Tier with me, hidden in my pocket, and cannot make myself give it up. If they did, they would change their minds about me. They would realize that the turtles must be my doing, wherever they come from and whether they mean good for us, or ill.

The knife seemed to twist as it came to her that the secret of the goozli was small compared to the other—the great, shameful secret that she had kept for so long. If Mab, Hara, Kay, Jewel and Sky knew that she was the daughter of Dare Larsett, they would see, as Britta now did herself, that Crow was right—that she was indeed the curse that had dogged the *Star of Deltora* from the beginning.

Her quest to become Mab's Apprentice had been doomed from the start—Britta knew that now. She had been a fool to think she could escape her past. Like her father, she had snatched at what she wanted in vanity and deceit. She had followed in Dare Larsett's footsteps, just as the *Star* had followed the route of his final voyage. And like Larsett, though without intending it, she had led her companions to disaster.

Numb with misery, she huddled in the prow, wishing with all her heart that Hara had put her over the side the moment the crew demanded it. She wished that Hara had not resisted Crow, wished that Mab had not spoken for her, that Jewel and Sky had not defended her. Then she would have been alone in her trouble—but her anguish would have been less.

Now that the oars had been shipped, the boat was moving smoothly. And, sure enough, it was not drifting aimlessly but gliding along in a definite direction, making good speed.

Britta could feel it, could hear Jewel gleefully pointing it out to the others, but she did not raise her head. She did not want to meet anyone's eyes. She did not want to see the turtles. Most of all, she did not want to be tempted to look over the leaden sea at the *Star of Deltora* growing smaller and smaller in the distance.

Jewel at last fell silent. No one else spoke. It

swam into Britta's exhausted mind that turtles or no turtles she and her companions would still be on the ship if Black Jack had not happened to cross her path. The sickening image of the cat's wild, golden eyes rose before her, and again a memory plucked at the edge of her mind, just out of reach.

It was no use. She could not think. It was becoming harder and harder to block out the whispers that hissed around her, endlessly repeating her father's name. It was easier simply to close her eyes, to give up the struggle, to let the whispers ebb and flow around her like the water rippling softly around the gliding boat.

For what seemed a very long time, Britta drifted in the space between sleep and waking. Pictures of Jantsy came to her there: Jantsy kneading bread in the warm bakery, looking up to smile a greeting, a smudge of flour on his cheek. Jantsy walking beside her at sunset, his honey-colored hair ruffled in the breeze. Jantsy waving a red scarf from the harbor shore, his white-clad figure growing smaller and smaller as the *Star of Deltora* surged towards the open sea ...

Faintly Britta could hear him whispering her name. *Britta ... Britta ... Britta ...* She smiled at the caressing sound, then her smile faltered. Jantsy had been shouting his farewell to her that day, not whispering! His hand had been cupped around his mouth. Borne on the wind, his voice had sounded as thin and wild as a seabird's call. It had not breathed softly into her mind, like this ...

Something was wrong. In her half sleep, Britta struggled to bring back the picture of Jantsy calling and waving from the shore. There he was, just as she remembered. Captain Gripp was beside him. Bosun, Gripp's polypan, was capering around them both …

Bosun!

And finally Britta grasped the memory that had been fluttering at the edge of her mind ever since she saw the terror in Black Jack's golden eyes. Suddenly she remembered the polypan bobbing and gibbering, baring his teeth at the sight of her, the evening that Gripp had told her about the Rosalyn contest. Bosun's eyes had blazed with fear that night—just as Black Jack's eyes had blazed this morning. And, like the cat, Bosun had not been looking directly at Britta, but at something behind her—something no one else could see.

Britta forced her heavy eyelids open. Shadows swooped and twined around her, so many that it was as if she was looking through a tattered gray veil. Adoring whispers flooded her unguarded mind, and amid the tumult of hissing sound she could hear two names repeated over and over again.

Britta … Britta … Larsett … Larsett … Larsett …

Memories … She caught at the word as if it were a lifeline, but it slipped away from her and vanished. She could believe in it no longer.

These voices sighing her father's name and her own could not be echoes from the past, stored in the timbers of the landing boat! Britta had never been in this boat before—and nor, she now remembered, had Dare Larsett! Her father had taken the *Star of Deltora*'s original landing boat to the Isle of Tier. This craft had been built to replace it.

The twining shadows were not memories either—suddenly Britta knew that. Suddenly she knew that the shadows, so much denser and more visible now than they had ever been before, were real. They were pressing close, wanting to be near her. She could sense their longing. She could feel their ghostly fingers brushing her face, her neck, her hair …

Dread took her by the throat. Through the tumult in her mind, she heard again the voice of the Del fortune-teller who called herself Lean Alice, croaking in the dark.

The girl has dealings with the dead in body, as well as the dead in spirit. I have seen them with her in this very street, attending her, fawning upon her, watching and listening …

They have been with me all along, Britta thought numbly. They have been haunting me since the day Captain Gripp told me of the Rosalyn contest. They boarded the *Star of Deltora* with me. They were with me in Maris harbor, in Two Moons, in the hold where I found the metal box, in Bar-Enoch's cavern … But why? What do they want of me?

Britta … Britta … Larsett's daughter … child of the Staff …

Britta made out the whispered words, and her blood ran cold. Frozen in horror, she gazed through the veil of flitting shadows at her companions in the boat.

Jewel was dozing, leaning against her oar with her head pillowed on her arms. Kay, Mab and Vashti were also asleep. Only Sky and Captain Hara were awake. Both of them sat motionless, looking past Britta at something ahead.

Stiffly, Britta turned to look over the prow. Between the boat and the horizon, the air was shimmering, rippling like water. The next moment, the illusion began fading like mist vanishing in sunlight. And as the terrible beauty it had hidden was revealed, she stopped breathing.

She had seen this sight before—or, rather, she had seen its image, embroidered on a silk wall hanging in a dim little shop on Two Moons. Then, she had not recognized it. She had not known why the image filled her with such passionate longing.

Now she understood. It had been the wraiths' yearning she had felt. And slowly, as she stared at what was ahead, the certainty grew in her that this was where her quest had always been fated to end.

An emerald island, wreathed in haze and ringed with black. Great seabirds wheeling silently above the haze. Ghostly shadows coiling like smoke from the lush forest, wavering on the glittering shore …

Tier—the Hungry Isle.

6 - The Glittering Shore

Britta felt the boat give a little jolt as the turtles began to swim more strongly, eager to reach their goal. She felt the goozli twitching in her pocket. She felt the excitement of the wraiths that seethed around her. Father has sent for me, she thought. And before she could guard against it, a stab of wild, foolish joy pierced her heart.

Sickened by her own weakness, she sat rigidly as the joy soured and cold dread crept back into the place where it had been. Dare Larsett had waded through blood to become the King of Tier. Now, it seemed, it pleased him to have his daughter's company, whether she wanted to join him or not. As for her companions …

Slowly she turned back to face Sky and Hara. They were no longer looking at the island, but at her. So were Mab, Kay and Jewel, who had been woken, perhaps, by the jerking of the boat.

She knew at once that they could all now see the wraiths surrounding her—knew it by their absolute stillness, by the horror in their eyes. Jewel's teeth were bared in revulsion. Sky's hand had closed around one of his braids, in the place where the charm that was supposed to ward off evil hung.

Britta's eyes burned. The wraiths pressed closer, moaning her name. Her living flesh shrank from their ghostly touch and she felt hot and cold by turns, as if she had a fever.

She forced her dry lips open. "I am sorry," she heard herself saying huskily. "I—did not know."

"Not ... your fault," Mab said faintly. "My fault—mine!" She plucked feverishly at the buttons of the tight jacket she had donned for Wrack's funeral.

"Be still, Mab." Kay seized the restless, quivering fingers and clasped them firmly. "Be still, my dear."

"More are coming," Sky said softly. "From the shore—over the water—do you see?" For once, his face was totally unguarded, and Britta could see that there was fascination in his eyes as well as fear. It came to her that many other people must have felt like Sky as they approached the Isle of Tier in ancient days. Their moaning shades flitted about her now.

A hideous vision of the future rose before her, and in that instant the clouds that filmed her mind parted and she saw clearly what she had to do.

She lurched sideways, intent on throwing herself into the sea. Hara's bellow echoed in her ears. Sky sprang forward and seized her around the waist, pulling her back to safety. Vashti woke, screaming.

"Let me go!" Britta cried, struggling frantically, cursing herself for being so stupid, so slow to realize what had to be done. "Without me you will have a chance to get away!"

In desperation she bit Sky's hand. He yelled in shock and, feeling his grip loosen, she tore herself free and scrambled for the side again.

"Hold her, Sky, curse you!" Hara roared.

"Do not listen to him!" Britta screamed, as Sky lunged for her and again dragged her back, this time sprawling with her into the bottom of the pitching boat. "Sky, for pity's sake! You have read enough to know what will happen if you are trapped on the island! The Staff will enslave you! You will become a wraith yourself! You and Jewel and—"

"I have read enough to know that letting you jump overboard will solve nothing!" Sky panted, holding her down. "We are inside the reef, Britta! It is too late for us to get away now—with you or without you. The Hungry Isle will have us if we try. It will destroy the boat and eat us alive. We must take our chances on the shore—we have no choice!"

And when Britta heard that, all the strength seemed to drain from her body. She stopped fighting and lay still, in blank despair.

Wraiths streamed from the beach and swarmed over the boat, more every moment. Vashti shrieked,

Jewel and Hara cursed, Mab groaned. But Sky made no sound, though pale, chill shadows brushed him jealously, trying to reach the girl pinned beneath him.

Britta felt the boat nudge the sand of the shore and come to rest. She felt Sky release his hold on her and sit up. She felt the bumps as people scrambled out into the shallow waves. She felt the boat being dragged out of the water, high onto the beach.

She felt it all, but she did not move—did not even raise her head. A rich perfume, headier by far than the scent she had noticed in the Two Moons swampland, was mingling with the smell of the warm seawater sloshing at the bottom of the boat. Her skin was prickling. Her ears were filled with adoring whispers.

Britta, the wraiths were whispering. *Larsett's daughter. You are home now, with us. With us …*

Britta heard, and shuddered. Words from *Mysteries of the Silver Sea* floated across the surface of her mind.

… the Staff bonds to the name and the flesh of its Master … the wraiths it has enslaved will worship that flesh and that name as they worship the Staff itself …

My father's blood runs in my veins, Britta thought. The wraiths sense it—that is why they want to be near me. For them, I am a link to the Staff that is everything to them. Poor, lost spirits …

How many times, in the safety of her bedroom in Del, had she shivered as she read in *A Trader's Life* of the unsuspecting travelers who had been lured to the Hungry Isle in its earliest days? So often that she knew the words by heart:

They came meaning only to spend an hour, but they never left. Becoming enraptured by the magic Staff, they stayed to worship it and fawn on its Master, while the island gorged first on their longboats, and then on their rotting ships.

By the Staff's power these poor wretches lived long in their bondage. But even when their hearts failed at last they remained as wraiths floating in the dim, perfumed air ...

The wraiths moaned, pressing closer. Britta felt their touch, like moths' wings brushing her skin, and recognized it. She had felt those caresses so often in the past weeks! Whenever she had been sad or angry, worried or afraid, the wraiths had drawn close to her and helplessly tried to comfort her. But then she had not known their touch for what it was, because she had seen them only as flickering shadows.

Now, on the island where their human lives had drained away so long ago, she could see their thin faces in the gray mist that swirled about her. She could see their slim, twining bodies. She could see their fluttering hands, whispering mouths and lost, hollow eyes. And she could feel that here they were stronger. Here they could act, where away from the island they could only watch and wait. Hope flared within her.

"Can you help us?" she cried. "Can you help us to get away from here?"

But the wraiths merely quivered in bewildered agitation and she saw in dismay that for them her question had no meaning. Their slavery to the Staff of Tier was complete. Their only happiness was to be near it, and to serve its Master. They could not imagine anyone feeling differently.

And there was something else. Britta realized it with desperate pity as the shades closed in around her again, softly chanting her name and her father's. In their pale half-life, the wraiths still faintly remembered what they had been. Once they had been flesh. Once they had had families and friends. Once they had loved.

For them there could be no hesitations, no doubts. Britta was Larsett's daughter—so of course she must want to be near him, just as he wanted to be near her. Nothing else was possible.

Britta caught her breath as another small flame of hope flickered to life within her. There might be little chance of escape for her, but surely there was a chance for the others. Her father had once loved her. If there was still a spark of feeling in the monster he had become …

Slowly she sat up. High on the curving black shore, before a background of lush forest, Jewel and

Sky were bending over Vashti, who was crouched on the sand with her head in her hands. Followed anxiously by Kay, Captain Hara was striding towards them with Mab cradled in his arms, threading his way through the huge, gleaming shells of basking turtles.

In many ways the scene looked very ordinary—like a picture in a story about a group of castaways. But of course, Britta thought grimly as she crawled to the side of the boat, I am seeing only half the picture. And she imagined what her companions on the shore were seeing—a disheveled girl in a flaring red skirt, surrounded by a throng of fawning ghosts. No wonder Sky and Jewel had fled from her as soon as they were able.

She quelled the wave of misery that threatened to engulf her. She had always been haunted by her past. The wraiths were just the visible sign of it. And now it suited her to be left alone with them. They would take her to her father.

The moment she set foot on the glittering sand, however, the wraiths' mood abruptly changed. They began writhing feverishly, hissing something new. Britta strained to make out the words.

We are summoned, Larsett's daughter. We must go to the cavern of the Staff. You must follow … follow …

For an instant they eddied around Britta like a whirlwind, nearly knocking her off her feet. Then they were gone, leaving her dizzy and blinking, swaying where she stood.

There were shouts, but they seemed very far away. Then she heard sand squeaking beneath a fast, heavy tread and felt a warm human hand gripping her arm, steadying her.

"So your admirers have left you, little nodnap," she heard Jewel say. "Where have they gone?"

"To—to their Master," Britta faltered. She could not bring herself to say, "to my father"—she simply could not. Looking up, she was astounded to see that Jewel was grinning.

"So we thought," Jewel said. "Well, we will follow their example. Mab —"

"No!" Britta cried. "I—I mean, *I* must follow them, but you—"

"Do not be ridiculous," Jewel broke in, beginning to hurry her towards the others. "Why should you face Larsett alone simply because his foul servants swarmed over you in the boat? It was just your bad luck that you were sitting in the prow, so were the first living creature they saw."

Britta's stomach turned over. Jewel thought that all the wraiths had come directly from the island—did not realize that some of them had been in the boat already.

Of course! The wraiths in the prow had only become visible when the island did, and more had rushed over the water just moments later. To Jewel, and to the others in the boat, it must have looked as if all the wraiths were part of the same invasion.

"And you tried to lead them overboard to save us—*then* held them in the boat while Hara and Kay got Mab safely away!" Jewel was exclaiming. "By the stars, Britta, I hope I would have had the same courage."

Britta cringed. "Jewel—" she began, but the words she might have said stuck in her throat.

"I am only sorry that I had to abandon you when we landed," Jewel rattled on. "Vashti bolted from the boat so wildly that it was all Sky and I could do to catch her."

She lifted her hand to Sky, who had moved with the others to stand by a dim gap between the forest trees. "A path leads into the forest just there, do you see? It could well be the way we must take."

Britta stumbled along in silence, not knowing what to do or say.

"Cheer up, little nodnap!" Jewel said, glancing at her. "We are in a tight place, certainly, but there is still a chance. Have you forgotten? Mab and Dare Larsett share a past. He was just a ragged boy when Mab helped him escape Del before the Shadowlands invasion. She helped him to become a successful trader—taught him everything she knew. He owes her a great deal. If she pleads for us he may agree to let us go, for her sake."

Britta nodded dully. In her turmoil, she *had* actually forgotten that her father and Trader Mab had a history that stretched back to a time long before she was born. She wet her lips. "But surely Mab is too weak to—"

"She seems a little better now she is on land," Jewel said. "She will have strength enough to plead our case, I think. *She* seems certain of it, at least, and she is impatient to make a start. So hurry on, Britta! We have to stay together—for our own safety, if for nothing else."

She glanced at Britta again, noted her grave expression, and grimaced. "Indeed! There can be no real safety here! But when danger threatens, what else can one do but whistle in the dark? And whether Mab succeeds or fails, at least when the thing is done the suspense will be over. At least we will *know*."

You will know more than you imagine, Jewel, Britta thought, her heart twisting in her chest. But still she said nothing, and soon it was too late to speak. They were reaching the gap in the trees, and her skin had begun to tingle. She could see the path winding away ahead of her and was seized with such a great longing to follow it that it was all she could do not to break into a run.

She moved into the green dimness, barely aware of Hara striding ahead of her with Mab in his arms, or of Jewel, Sky, Kay and Vashti following behind. The silent call was very strong. She could feel it in every fiber of her being. And she obeyed it without thought and almost without fear, though she knew in her bones that it was not her father who was summoning her, but the magic Staff of Tier.

7 - The Cavern

Haze drifted in the treetops above them, masking the sky. Orchids with petals like flabby, speckled flesh hung heavily from knotted boughs, their powerful scent reminding Britta of the smell of overripe fruit. Ferns grew tall and rank between vast, twisted roots, and thick tongues of purple fungus poked from the rotting stumps of fallen trees. There was no sound but the sullen gurgle of slowly running water.

"It should be beautiful, but it is not," Jewel muttered to Sky. "There is—a wrongness in it."

"Indeed," Sky answered bleakly. "According to the old tales, it was a paradise when Tier created it, and was still beautiful in the time of Bar-Enoch. The magic has soured since then, it seems. Perhaps Dare Larsett's mastery of the Staff is not as perfect as it might be."

"I would keep such thoughts to myself, if I were

you," Jewel breathed. "My thumbs are pricking. There is menace here—just waiting its time."

Britta heard their voices, but the words had no more meaning for her than the gurgling of the stream. The cavern of the Staff was very near—she could feel it. Her heart was thudding painfully. Her whole body was tingling. *Soon ... soon ...*

The path curved around a vast tree so infested with orchids hanging layer upon layer from its boughs that its trunk was invisible. And there, straight ahead, was a wall of dull black rock. In the wall a great mouth gaped, fringed with rusty moss and filled with a swirling mass of tiny silver stars. A whispering sound drifted through the glittering veil, as if the cavern itself were breathing.

Hara stopped dead. Mab murmured to him and he set her down. She turned to Britta.

"I would like you to help me on from here, Britta, if you are willing," she said, her voice surprisingly strong. "The island's wraiths have made a bond with you, and their goodwill may be of value. Hara and the others can stay here and wait."

No one said a word. Britta caught a single glimpse of Jewel's frozen face, of Sky's crooked grin, of Vashti's dull stare and Kay's worried frown. Then Mab's hand had fastened on her arm, and they were walking together, with painful slowness, towards the cavern.

"Mab," Britta made herself say as the old trader stopped to gasp for breath, "there is no need for you—"

"There is every need!" Mab snapped. "Thanks to that scoundrel Crow, things have not happened as I planned, but I have spent two long years waiting for this moment and I cannot turn back now."

Britta gaped at her, dumbfounded.

Mab scowled. "Have you not guessed it yet, girl? Have you not guessed why we gave our usual crew leave and hired less able and intelligent hands for this voyage? Or why our last port was Illica, where the trading is chancy at the best of times?"

When Britta still stared, she shrugged in disgust. "Well, you would have found me out in a minute or two in any case, so we might as well get it over now. The fact is, Tier has been my goal from the beginning. Its last reported sighting was southeast of Illica, and Hara was secretly steering the ship towards it when Crow made his move. I needed to come here, Britta. I have something to ask of your father."

Britta's throat closed. Her face and neck were suddenly burning hot.

"Oh yes," Mab said dryly. "I know who you are. I have been hearing news of you for a long time—Captain Gripp has no secrets from me. I promised him silence, and I kept my word. Your visits made the old man happy, and what did I care what you did? But then—then I found a use for you. So I told Gripp to sponsor you for the Rosalyn contest."

"*You!* But –"

Mab's mouth twisted into a grim smile. "The

contest was the best excuse I could think of to take an unknown girl like you on a voyage without raising suspicion at the Traders' Hall. And I needed you as protection—and bait."

Bait. Britta's mind was spinning. She could not speak.

"We knew roughly where to find the Hungry Isle," Mab went on harshly. "Our problem was how to make the island show itself, and stop it attacking the *Star*. You were the answer to that. Your father doted on you. I was sure that he would not be able to resist seeing you if you were near. And so it has proved."

The scalding sense of betrayal was almost more than Britta could bear. "Captain Gripp *knew*—?"

The old woman snorted. "Gripp knew only what I told him—that I wanted to do you a good turn in secret, help you towards a life as a trader if I could. As it was, I had to delay announcing the contest till you were old enough for Gripp to feel happy about sponsoring you—delay, I might say, that I could ill afford."

As if her final words had spurred her on, she started forward again. Britta was forced to walk with her, though she longed to shake off the bony hand that gripped her arm so tightly.

"I am dying," Mab said abruptly. "Crow was right about that, curse him, just as he was right about the ship's being off course. For two years I have known that all Kay's skill could not slow the cursed disease that has its claws in me. Only a miracle can save me—and the Staff that cures all ills is that miracle. The Staff can heal me. I am not ready to die. Dare Larsett owes me a great deal. It is as simple as that."

As simple as that. Britta stared ahead, her mind numb.

"I was perfectly prepared to distort the test results, if necessary, to make sure you would be a finalist," Mab added, glancing sideways at her. "But as it happened the tie between you, Jewel and Sky was the only real problem I faced. Sorrel took a fancy to you—and you are not without talent."

Perhaps she felt that this crumb of comfort would help. In a way, it did, though Britta despised herself for the small rush of pleasure it gave her.

They stopped at the cave entrance. The whispers of the wraiths, heavy with longing, gusted through the mist of whirling, glittering stars. Britta could sense nothing of her father. She could only feel the magic of the Staff that had possessed him.

"Dare!" Mab called softly. "Dare Larsett!"

Leaning heavily on Britta's arm she took a step forward, into the mist. The cavern seemed to tremble. "It is Mab, Dare!" she called a little more strongly. "It is Mab, the Trader Rosalyn. I have come to beg—"

There was a brilliant flash of light and a hissing sound. With a scream of agony, Mab crumpled to the ground.

The cries of Hara, Kay and the others rang in

Britta's ears as she fell to her knees beside Mab, the call of the Staff suddenly banished from her mind. The old trader's eyes were closed. Her mouth hung slightly open. Her face was gray. There was a black, burned patch on her temple.

"Leave her, Britta," a cracked voice whispered through the mist. "I have put an end to her. She had no business here. You are the one I have been waiting for."

Britta shivered all over. This was not the warm, rich voice of the father she had loved. It was rasping, as if it was seldom used. Worse than that, it sounded flat and dead. A stone statue made to speak might have had such a voice. And in that instant Britta knew that the mind behind the voice was just as changed, just as drained of humanity.

The croaking being in this cavern was no longer the dashing Dare Larsett, no longer her laughing father. He was Larsett, Master of the Staff, Larsett, King of Tier.

Mab had not realized that. For once, Mab had made an error. She had trusted in the memory of old friendship, and she had been struck down with the words "I have come to beg" on her lips.

I must not make the same mistake, Britta thought grimly, with the one small, cold part of her mind not paralyzed by shock and dread. I must not trust in his love. I must not plead. Somehow I must find a way to bargain.

She grimaced as words from *A Trader's Life* floated into her mind, taunting her.

You will make your best trades when you have taken the trouble to learn the strengths and weaknesses of your trading partner ...

Weaknesses? What chinks could she possibly find in the armor of the King of Tier, Master of an ancient sorcerer's Staff that could create and destroy, could grant eternal life?

Then Hara was by her side, pushing her roughly out of the way, crouching beside Mab's body. Healer Kay was close behind him. And as Britta scrambled to her feet, she saw that Jewel and Sky had also plunged heedlessly into the sparkling mist.

In horror, she felt the cavern begin to tremble once more.

"Do not harm them!" she cried out, forgetting her resolution completely. "They are my friends!"

The whispers hissing beyond the mist rose to a gale, and a desolate moaning began, dying away only as the ominous trembling ceased.

The wraiths made him stop, Britta thought numbly. The wraiths care for me, and they made him stop! They have some power over him, then. They may be his slaves, but for some reason he does not want to upset them. That is a weakness.

And as she tucked that scrap of knowledge away in her mind, she suddenly remembered that in fact the wraiths had never been the slaves of any person. The tales all made it clear that wraiths were the slaves of the

Staff itself! They did her father's bidding only because he had claimed the magic object that had enthralled them so long ago.

And what had Sky said in the forest? Britta had paid no attention to his words at the time, but now they floated into her mind and clung there.

Perhaps Dare Larsett's mastery of the Staff is not as perfect as it might be.

If this were true, it would explain the King's caution in his dealings with the wraiths. Another weakness …

"How could you do this, Larsett?" Hara shouted, looking up from Mab's body, his eyes gleaming with tears. "She trusted you! You owed her so much!"

"Ha!" A grating laugh echoed through the cavern. "So here is another poor fool hypnotized by Mab! Another pet dog who has allowed himself to be used in return for crumbs dropped from the Trader Rosalyn's table! Old Gripp was one such dolt. Trader Sorrel, too. And so was I—till I grew sick of my gilded kennel and took my fate into my own hands."

Larsett, sighed the wraiths. *Larsett, Master of the Staff …* The silver sparks swirling in the air shivered and danced madly as the cracked voice came again.

"Mab never gave me the respect I deserved. She jeered at my dreams. She told me to stay in my place. But look at her now—a painted crone, dead by my will, while rubies pour from my fingertips and life surges within me as strongly as ever."

Hara made a strangled sound. In terror, Britta saw his fists clench and the muscles of his arms and shoulders bunch beneath the fabric of his coat.

Do not move, Captain Hara, she implored him silently. *Do not give him any excuse …*

Kay gripped Hara's sleeve, whispering urgently. Hara seemed to struggle with himself for a moment, then his shoulders relaxed.

Britta breathed out, weak with relief. She heard Jewel sigh behind her, but resisted the urge to look round.

Her companions' safety was in her hands now. She had to concentrate on helping them escape the Hungry Isle. She must think of nothing else.

Coldly, Britta cleared her mind. She put aside her horror at Mab's death. She put aside her old, childish yearning for the father she had loved and lost. She put aside her shrinking at the thought of her companions learning who she was. She put aside her dread.

"Have you nothing to say to me, Britta?" the King of Tier demanded impatiently. "Has the story of my triumph turned even you against me?"

His voice rose. "The puny minds of Del think ill of me. My name is cursed among the common herds of the Silver Sea. I have been aware of that for a very long time. But surely *you* know that I did only what I had to do, to rise to glory? After all these years, have you nothing to say to your loving father?"

8 - Time to Trade

Britta heard Jewel curse in shock. She heard Kay give a small, smothered cry. Sky and Hara made no sound at all, but she could imagine their blank, closed faces. And no doubt Vashti was crouched somewhere outside the cavern, her hand pressed to her mouth, her eyes wide with disgusted horror. The King had spoken quite loudly enough for the sound to carry into the clearing.

So that is that, Britta thought. Now they know.

Strangely, it was almost a relief.

"It is hard to know what to say," she said steadily. "I thought I would never see you again. I did not expect you to send for me."

"I did not send for you!" The denial burst angrily through the mist. The sparks of light spun and flashed. The wraiths hissed in agitation. Britta stood her ground, adding another scrap of knowledge to her small store.

"I did not send for you, Britta," the King resumed more calmly. "For the first time since gaining my kingdom, I ordered wraiths to bring me news of you, but that is all. Fate has brought you here—fate, and the noble Trader Rosalyn, who used you as a lure and a shield to force her way into my presence."

Again the stars danced madly as he struggled to control his anger. Again the wraiths sighed and moaned.

"Oh, yes—I heard!" he went on at last. "I heard what she said to you. But what does it matter? Mab has been punished for deceiving you, and you are here—the beloved daughter I thought I had lost forever."

There was tension in his voice. Britta could hear it plainly, but she could not understand it. In fact, there were many things she did not understand. None of her father's words rang true.

Her stomach lurched. Could it be that he was speaking for the wraiths' benefit—saying the things *they* expected of him? The next words made her almost sure that she was right.

"Tier has opened its arms to you, Britta. The wraiths of the island feel your bond with me, with the hand that holds the Staff of life and death. They want you here with us—and of course I feel the same."

"What of my companions?" Britta asked. Behind her, Jewel and Sky tensed.

"No human has ever escaped the Hungry Isle alive—you surely know that, Britta. Your companions can stay and join the wraiths in time, or they can try to leave and let their bodies feed the island. It is all one to us."

Swallowing the cry of entreaty that rose in her throat, Britta focused on those last words. *It is all one to us.* Not *to me*, but *to us*. It was a message, she was sure of it.

"We sense that you are unhappy, my little Britta," the rusty voice croaked on as the wraiths moaned softly in the sparkling mist. "The wraiths are saddened and confused. They cannot understand why you do not feel pure joy in the presence of the Staff and your loving father. Will you tell us what is troubling you?"

Britta fought down a wave of nausea. However changed her father was, he must surely know that the last thing in the world she wanted was to stay with him in this enchanted, timeless prison, watching her friends die.

He did know it, perfectly well. The strain in the cracked voice told her that. So did his stiff, formal speech, so different from the confident, casual way of speaking that she remembered.

But the wraiths were fretting because she was not happy. And the great King of Tier did not like to upset them.

Very well, Father, Britta thought grimly. It is time for us to bargain.

Deliberately she breathed out, willing her tense muscles to relax. "I am sad for my friends," she said, taking care to speak simply and clearly so the wraiths would hear and understand. "My friends did not ask to come here, and they have their own lives to live. I care for them deeply. I could never have another moment's happiness if they died or lost their freedom because of me."

As this was the honest truth, it was not difficult for her to sound earnest. By the time she had finished, her voice was shaking. Swallowing the lump in her throat, she heard the wraiths sighing in sympathy.

Good, she thought. They grieve for me. Surely now he will have to offer to let the others go, for my sake. She held her breath, waiting for the response.

But when it came, it was not what she had expected.

"I cannot believe that your sadness is only for your friends," the King hissed. "Speak your mind, Britta! Forget your trader's tricks for once and tell me what you want for yourself."

Britta hesitated, her mind running in circles. Should she tell the truth? Would it harm her companions, or would it help them?

She jumped as a hand touched her shoulder. Then Sky was muttering urgently in her ear.

"He is looking for a way to let you go, Britta! Do you not hear it in his voice? He just has to convince the wraiths that he has good reason to send you away!"

Britta felt the hot blood rush into her face. Was Sky right? Did her father still feel enough, still love her enough, to want her to be free?

I did not send for you!

The denial had been very fast, very abrupt, as if it had burst from her father's throat on a wave of strong feeling. Remembering it now, it seemed to her that there had been a note of desperation in it.

Perhaps it had been the only truly heartfelt thing he had said from the beginning.

Britta felt her emotions seesawing wildly. Love—hate, pity—rage, joy—grief, hope—fear, trust—suspicion …

Instinctively she glanced down at Mab's body, cradled in Hara's arms. Her heart leaped as she saw a bright gleam beneath Mab's eyelashes. Mab's eyes were open, though she was keeping them veiled. Mab was alive—alive and aware!

Kay and Hara must know it by now. But they had not betrayed their knowledge by a single look or sign. They knew that while Mab was playing dead, she was safe.

Like Captain Mikah, Britta thought suddenly, remembering the chilling message that had been found with the valiant captain's bones on the drifting *Star of Deltora*. The Staff had struck Mikah down but he had survived—long enough, at least, to make sure that the truth did not die with him.

How strange that the mighty Master of the Staff should make the same mistake twice! He had left the *Star of Deltora* believing that he had killed everyone aboard, but later he must have realized his error. He claimed to have known for a long time that his name was cursed in Del and throughout the Silver Sea. So he must have realized that someone had survived to tell of what he had done—for how else could the story of his guilt have spread?

Yet still he took it for granted that Mab was dead. Still he did not doubt his power to kill outright when he chose.

Britta's scalp prickled.

"Well, Daughter?" the cracked voice demanded impatiently. "Will you not answer me? What do you want for yourself?"

Fighting for calm, Britta clamped her trembling hands together. She had to speak. But what should she say? Mab's eyes widened very slightly, and Britta caught another brief, bright gleam, directed straight at her.

Trust your instincts …

Carefully expressionless, Britta looked up and stared blindly into the starry mist. "I am still young," she said slowly, "and I feel that my real life, the life I was born to lead, has only just begun. I have always longed to be a trader—to sail the nine seas, to see new places and meet people who are different from the people at home."

"I remember," said the King of Tier, a strange note in his rasping voice. "And as I recall, I told you that when the time came I would help you do it. Are you saying that you wish to hold me to that promise, Britta?"

Whispers gusted like a gentle wind from the depths of the cavern. The silver stars circled and spun before Britta's eyes.

Her throat tightened. "Yes," she answered. "If I could choose, I would choose to be free. The—the world is wide, and full of wonders."

She waited, her whole body throbbing with tension. She could feel Jewel and Sky behind her holding their breath. Beside her, Hara, Mab and Kay were as still as stones.

"Then, Britta, we will make a trade," the King said, so quickly that she was certain he had been waiting impatiently for his chance to say the words. "My part of the bargain is something that only I can give you—your freedom, and the freedom of your companions."

Britta dug her nails into her palms to force herself not to speak. There was a dull roaring in her ears. Her head was spinning with a confusion of shock, dread and piercing joy.

"Your part is—" the ruined voice trembled, paused, then went on more strongly, "—your part is something that only you can give me."

Instantly, Britta thought of the goozli. Perhaps the wraiths had brought news of it to the cavern. Perhaps the Staff had sensed its presence. And of course the King would want it. It had been made by the ancient magic of the turtle man Tier, who had created the Staff, who had made this island live long ago. Of course …

She touched her pocket and felt the goozli stir beneath her hand. The warmth of the little creature's loyalty and trust flowed through her fingers. She was bonded to the goozli. Fate had delivered it into her hands, and she had kept it by her through all her troubles. But if it was the price of freedom for her and the others, she would have to give it up. Of course she would, though the very thought wrung her heart.

But as she opened her mouth to make the offer, familiar words from *A Trader's Life* made her think again.

Do not show your hand too soon. Make your trading partner state what he or she wants of you, or you may find yourself offering more than you need to do …

"What is it, that only I can give you?" she made herself ask.

She had braced herself for the answer, but when it came it was so unexpected, yet at the same time so entirely what she *should* have expected, that her knees seemed to turn to water.

"I want to hear you call me 'Father' once more," the creaking voice said softly. "I want your farewell kiss, to comfort me in my loneliness. And then, Britta, however hard it may be, I want you to turn away without another word, and forget me."

"Forget ..." Britta echoed through dry lips.

"You and your companions may go only if you swear this, on your life. You must forget whose daughter you are. You must forget what has passed between us this day. You must put me out of your mind, and never speak my name again to any living soul. This solemn promise, made on your honor as a Del trader, must be part of our bargain, for without it you will never be truly free."

The wraiths sighed in loving, mournful pity. *Larsett,* they whispered, like dry leaves rustling. *Larsett ...*

"Do we understand each other, Britta?" asked the King of Tier. "Do we have a bargain?"

Britta was trembling all over now. She felt very cold. "Yes," she said.

Feeling the eyes of her companions boring into the back of her neck, she stepped forward. The starry mist thinned and vanished.

The great cavern was revealed in all its splendor. Rainbow light radiated from the gem-studded walls, coloring the twining wraiths, playing on the face of the being seated on a golden throne, gripping a tall, black Staff.

He looked no older than he had looked when Britta had last seen him on the deck of the *Star of Deltora,* over eight years ago. But he was no longer a man like other men. The pale skin that covered his wasted frame glowed faintly blue, as if he were a creature of the deep, and his eyes were deep black pools that did not reflect the light. The rich fabric of his scarlet robe flowed in liquid folds from his shoulders and pooled like blood around his feet.

Britta stared at the mighty King of Tier and saw a shriveled soul in a crimson shroud. There was a great thundering in her ears. She looked at the hand that held the Staff and saw the flesh twitch beneath the glimmering skin as the Staff leaned very slightly towards her. Words that she had seen carved in the death chamber of the pirate Bar-Enoch burned in her mind.

BY THE MAGIC OF THE TURTLE
MAN THE STAFF FIRST CAME TO ME.
IT KNOWS MY FLESH. IT KNOWS MY NAME.
IT CLEAVES TO ME ALONE.

The straining fingers tightened on the Staff. A red spark flickered in the depths of the dead eyes. The right hand rose, and beckoned. Britta forced herself to move, forced her trembling legs to carry her step-by-step to the golden throne.

"Father," she said, and the wraiths twined around her sadly, lovingly, as she bent to kiss the offered cheek that was as smooth and cold as a gravestone.

"Go now," the King said, turning his head away. "And tell your friends to take their dead with them."

9 - The Path

Britta did not remember leaving the cavern. She came to herself stumbling back along the forest path, supported by Healer Kay, with Captain Hara on her other side, Mab a dead weight in his arms.

The wraiths had not followed. Perhaps they had been ordered to stay where they were. Or perhaps they had chosen to remain with the Staff and to twine about the King, praising his sacrifice.

A feeling of desolation, loss and waste settled over Britta like a heavy cloak. Her heart felt as if it had been turned to stone.

You must forget whose daughter you are. You must forget what has passed between us this day. You must put me out of your mind, and never speak my name again to any living soul ...

Jewel, Sky and Vashti were hurrying along together a little way ahead. Now and again they disappeared from view as the path curved. Britta wondered if they were talking about her—talking of the shameful secret she had kept from them. Vashti's horror and spite she could easily imagine, but what of Jewel and Sky? She had saved them by the bargain she had struck, but they would never know what it had cost her.

A soft moan escaped Britta's lips. Healer Kay glanced at her quickly then looked away, her face taut with anger.

"How could you do it?" Kay muttered. "It was wicked—monstrous! Do not pretend you did not know it!"

Britta did not even try to reply. Then Hara spoke, and with a shock she realized that Kay had not been talking to her at all, but to him!

"I am past pretending, Kay," Hara growled, brushing aside a trailing orchid that dangled over the path. "Nothing matters now. Of course I knew who the girl was! Why do you think I ignored the Keeper's warning in Maris? Because I was sure he was sensing Britta's bond with Larsett and the Staff! We kept the facts from you because Mab thought you'd react just as you have done. She knew you wouldn't see reason, and she needed you."

"Reason!" hissed Kay. "Blind selfishness, you mean! To search for the Isle of Tier was one thing—though frankly I never thought we would find it. But to take Britta from her home, to deceive her so cruelly, to put her in such appalling danger—"

"Mab said that Larsett loved the girl," Hara said sullenly. "She was sure he would not keep her with him unless she wished it."

"Mab was sure of many things about Larsett," snapped Kay, glancing down at the ugly burn on the old trader's temple. "Too many." And suddenly tears welled up in her eyes and ran down her cheeks.

Britta looked down. She stared blankly at the flounce of her red skirt, swinging softly against her boot tops as she walked. In slow wonder she remembered how happy she had been when she put the skirt on for the first time. Only a few days had passed since she stood admiring her reflection in the mirror of that dressmaker's shop in Illica. It seemed years.

"This is no time to despair, Kay," she heard Hara mutter. "We cannot be far from the shore now. If Larsett keeps his word and luck is with us, we—"

His voice broke off in a choking cry. At the same moment, Kay yelled in alarm. Britta's head jerked up. She looked round, and thrilled with horror.

Hara was staggering backward, clawing at his neck, with Mab still clutched awkwardly in one arm. Something was bobbing between his fingers—a hideous, flabby creature as big as his hand, with a gaping, speckled throat …

Not a creature—an orchid! The cloying smell of it gusted into Britta's face, turning her stomach, as she sprang to Hara's aid, shouting for Jewel and Sky.

Bruised petals spilled onto Hara's chest, onto Mab's body, onto the ground. Hara had torn the flower apart, but he could not break the long stem, tough as rope, that had stretched from an overhanging branch to wind tightly around his neck. He had managed to slide two fingers under the stem and was straining it away from his throat, just enough to give him a little air. But he was weakening. His knees were sagging. His breath came in shallow, wheezing gasps.

"We are betrayed!" cried Kay, frantically hauling at the stem to try to break it. "Ah, what will become of us? Take Mab, Britta! Make haste!"

Mab was already slipping from Hara's grip. It was easy to pull her free. But bone thin as the old woman was, she was still surprisingly heavy. All Britta could do was cushion her fall as they both tumbled backward onto the ground.

Stunned and winded, Britta sat up, gasping for breath. Her head was spinning, and pinpoints of light danced before her eyes. Mab had rolled out of her arms and was sprawled on the damp earth beside her like a discarded rag doll. A few paces away, Kay was still struggling to help Hara, but Britta could hardly hear the healer's voice. Her ears were suddenly filled with a strange, liquid, hissing sound that she did not recognize, but which seemed to be all around her.

Something as cold and flabby as a drowned man's hand brushed her cheek. She screamed and batted it away, her heart pounding wildly.

And there, swinging slowly away from her, was another huge, dangling festoon of orchids. Clumps of flesh-colored petals wriggled horribly along the ropelike stem. Dark-spotted throats gaped.

The tip of the stem slapped the ground and instantly writhed towards Mab. At the same moment, a great tongue of purple fungus pushed up from the earth of the path and pressed hungrily against the old trader's neck.

"Jewel!" Britta screamed, seizing Mab's shoulders and struggling to drag her out of danger. "Sky! Help!"

No one answered. No feet pounded towards her. All Britta could hear was the gurgling, hissing sound that seemed to be growing louder, louder …

She twisted her neck to look around her, and what she saw turned her heart to ice. In the few seconds that had passed since she fell, the entire path, except the small patch where she crouched with Mab, had become a thrashing sea of orchids.

A sickening odor rose from the heaving, hissing mass. Every moment more ropey stems snaked out from the forest floor and reached down from overhanging branches. Every moment more quivering tongues of fungus erupted from the quaking earth.

Sky and Vashti were staggering, waist deep, in tangling thongs of vine that were slowly dragging them off the path. Jewel was the only one moving freely. She was fighting furiously, something bright gleaming in her hand as she turned and slashed through a stem that was snaking around Sky's neck. Somehow Jewel had found a weapon. What—?

And then Britta saw what the gleaming object was. It was Jewel's armband—the gold armband that had so impressed Madam Bell-Slink in Illica. Its razor-sharp edges were slicing through the strangling stems like butter. Jewel was wielding it ferociously, expertly, as if she had been trained to fight with it from her earliest days.

As, of course, she had, Britta realized in dazed wonder. The armband was Jewel's secret weapon—a weapon disguised as a handsome ornament, never to be used except in a matter of life and death.

Jewel was using it now, to save herself, to save Sky and Vashti, to cleave her way back to Britta, Mab, Hara and Kay. But even Jewel could not fight a whole forest—a whole, hungry island. Sooner or later even her great strength would fail, and then …

With a thrill of horror, Britta felt something plucking at her sleeve. But when she looked down, she could only see Mab's fingertips, feebly tugging the bright silk. The old trader's eyes were open. She was trying to say something. Britta bent till her ear was close to the dry lips.

"He … has broken the bargain," she heard Mab breathe. "You … are no longer bound. Go back! Only you can stop …"

The whisper faded. The bony hand fell heavily to the ground.

Her heart swelling till it seemed it would burst, Britta staggered to her feet. Out of the corner of her eye she saw a stem bobbing with orchids snaking eagerly towards Mab. With a cry she swung round.

"Leave me, girl!" Mab croaked. "Do what you must! I order you!"

Britta ran. She heard Kay shouting after her, screaming to her to stop, but she did not look back.

Fate has brought you here … Fate has brought you here … The words hammered in her mind as she ran, her eyes fixed on the path ahead, her stomach boiling with the bitterness of grief and betrayal. She ran as she had never run in her life before, dodging the wagging pillars of fungus that jutted from the churned earth, crushing orchids beneath her feet.

Only when she reached the great tree where the path ended, and paused to gasp for breath, did she wonder how she had managed to come so far without being brought down. The trailing orchids that shrouded the tree were rearing, hissing and thrashing like serpents, but most did not reach for her, and those that did recoiled at her touch.

She started violently as something knocked against her leg, then realized that it was only the goozli, twitching violently in her skirt pocket. The little creature wanted to help her, no doubt, but it was safer where it was.

She pressed her hands to her aching chest, trying to calm her ragged breathing, trying not to think of what might be happening to Mab, to Hara, to Kay. She had to be able to speak when she entered the cavern—and speak loudly and clearly too. She would not have much time.

Still the orchids on the tree kept back. Still they did not strike. It seemed that she alone was immune to the attack of the Hungry Isle. She shuddered at the thought that her bond with her father, with the Staff of Tier, might be keeping her safe.

Larsett's daughter … child of the Staff …

It was horrible, horrible! She could not bear it! Again a picture of Bar-Enoch's vain boast swam before her eyes, more completely this time.

BY THE MAGIC OF THE TURTLE
MAN THE STAFF FIRST CAME TO ME.
IT KNOWS MY FLESH. IT KNOWS MY NAME.
IT CLEAVES TO ME ALONE. SHOULD I GROW
WEARY OF THIS LIFE, MY DEATH WILL NOT
DIVIDE US. ANY LIVING SOUL WHO TRIES TO
TAKE IT FROM ME WILL BE SLAIN.

And suddenly, understanding burst into Britta's mind, burning like flame. For an instant she stood motionless as a wave of heat surged through her body to the very tips of her fingers.

Then she bent and unbuttoned the heaving pocket. The goozli shot out into her hand. With high, bubbling hisses, the orchids shrank away from it.

"So it is you they fear, goozli," Britta said softly. "I was not protecting you—you were protecting *me*. And it was because you were close by that Mab was not killed outright by the Staff—is that not so?"

The little clay figure bowed, and waited.

It came to Britta that now she had a choice. She did not have to enter the cavern and face what waited for her there. Instead, she could run back to the others with the goozli in her hand, and lead them through the forest to the shore. She could trust that the goozli's magic, the pure, unchanged magic of the turtle man Tier, would be powerful enough to calm the waters of the Hungry Isle, and carry the landing boat across the reef, into the open sea.

Almost, she was tempted. But then she looked at the misty cavern mouth ahead. She thought of the father she had loved so much, lost to her forever. She thought of the king of lies who crouched beyond the mist—the cold, croaking sorcerer who had asked for a kiss and then betrayed her, as he had betrayed so many others who had trusted him.

She curled her fingers around the goozli and held it to her cheek, whispering to it softly. Then she set it down on the ground.

"Whatever happens to me, do what you can for

the others," she breathed, barely moving her lips. "For my sake, goozli!"

The goozli's eyes were grave. Sadly it shook its head and touched its brow and its chest. Britta could only hope that it had understood.

She thought she could hear it scuttling close behind her as she crept quickly and quietly to the cavern mouth, but she could not be sure. Agitated whispers were drifting from the starry mist. The wraiths were chanting her name.

Britta, Britta, Britta ...

"Be still, curse you!" an angry voice rasped. "You must stay here, to comfort me in my grief, until—until it pleases me to let you go. Your senses are deceiving you, I tell you! By now my daughter and her friends are safely at sea. If they were in danger I, the Master of the Staff, would know it!"

White-hot rage took Britta by the throat. Suddenly it was not hard to do what she had to do.

"Liar!" she shouted, running blindly into the mist. "You are not—"

With a sharp crack, flame shot from the center of the cavern like a bolt of lightning. The whirling stars vanished. Flung backward by the blast, Britta fell senseless to the ground. The wraiths howled piteously.

And in the shadows the goozli raised its head, then moved to do what it could.

10 - Fate

The King of Tier sat trembling on his golden throne, wraiths flying about his head like wailing smoke. The shock had left him feeling empty, and feeble as a child. He looked at the body of the girl lying on the cavern floor and a cold, yawning hollow seemed to open in his chest.

He had fully intended to keep his part of the bargain and let the intruders go. Why else had he made Britta swear to forget him? But once he had what he wanted, once the wraiths were content, he had thought again.

Was the Master of the Staff, the King of Tier, to be bound by a common trader's oath? The very thought had angered him. Had he not said at the beginning that no one escaped the Hungry Isle?

Suddenly it had begun to seem weak and foolish to keep his promise, when he could choose to do otherwise. And as time went by it had seemed to him more and more likely that Britta was thinking the same thing. So he had sent the command for the forest to feed, to kill.

But then Britta had returned to the cavern raging, accusing ... and in panic he had struck her down.

He had killed many times before, but this death was different. Something had ended for him when Britta fell—he could feel it. It was as if he had crossed an invisible line, as if from this point on there would be no turning back.

Yet surely there had never been a chance of turning back. From the moment he saw the Staff of Tier, from the moment he felt its power and knew that he had to possess it at any cost, his fate had been sealed.

The wraiths swooped around him, wild in their mourning, bright as exotic birds in the rainbow light. Their grief had made them daring. The King knew he had to quell them. He roused himself.

"You are to blame for this!" he rasped. "If you had not angered me, it would never have happened! Plainly my daughter had changed her mind. She was coming back to me—to be with me always! And because you had distracted me I struck at her blindly, thinking she was a stranger. Cease your wretched howling! Your grief can be nothing to mine! Nothing!"

The wraiths moaned, their eyes dark pits in their gaunt, rainbow-painted faces. Images of Britta had begun flickering among them. Some the King had seen before. Others he had not. He gnawed his lips as the images appeared and vanished, appeared and vanished: Britta behind the counter of a shop in Del. Britta on the deck of the *Star of Deltora*. Britta struggling in the mud of the Two Moons swamp. Britta smiling at a little clay doll balanced on the palm of her hand. Britta reading words carved on a smooth rock wall. Britta bending to kiss a cold cheek. Britta bursting through the mist, her eyes flashing. Britta falling …

The King tasted blood on his lips. He closed his eyes, but the last two images still glowed inside his eyelids as if they had been burned there.

The wraiths would cease their wailing in time. The Staff would soon consume their attention once more. A few weeks, months, years … and all this would be forgotten—all but the most important thing.

The King's mouth twitched wryly. Even he would forget, no doubt, as his memories of this day sank in the endless, silent oceans of time. But for now …

He forced the stiff fingers that held the Staff of Tier to tighten, forced the images of Britta back, forced his thoughts away from the body on the floor. He had to focus on the forest path, to make sure that the feeding frenzy he had set in motion would continue with all possible speed.

Keeping his eyes shut he concentrated, taking care to shield his mind. A picture of the writhing forest came to him, more dimly than usual but clear enough to startle him. One of the intruders—the woman of

Broome—was fighting the attack! She had some sort of weapon, though the Staff had clearly shown him that she had carried nothing onto the island.

There were other survivors too, gathered in a tight knot behind her. The King could not see them clearly, could not see how many of them there were, but they were all on their feet, that was certain.

The King hesitated. He knew that it would be prudent to keep to his plan and take no active part in destroying the invaders of his peace. The wraiths might detect a killing spell, and their faith in him had been shaken enough. Besides, there was no doubt that the forest would prevail in the end.

Yet the thought that his will was being defied made fury rise in him. What was more, though the wraiths' dismal whining tormented him, he could not order them to leave the cavern till all traces of the intruders had vanished beneath the island's greedy earth. He did not dare.

He, the all-powerful King of Tier, did not dare ...

His rage swelled. He could feel the hot blood pulsing in the veins of his neck. The shadowy picture he held in his mind wavered then suddenly grew clearer. Now he could see that the wretches sheltering behind the woman of Broome were supporting one another, defending their tight circle as best they could, beating back crawling orchids with belt buckles, boots—even with what looked like huge gold coins. And among them ... among them ...

At first he could not believe it. He told himself that the flare of red in the center of the group was a mirage. But then he saw, beneath that blazing crest of hair, the fierce, haggard face, the narrowed eyes like chips of flint …

Mab! But Mab was dead! He had killed her! With his own eyes he had seen her crumpled lifeless on the cavern floor.

Yet there Mab stood—feeble but alive, held upright by that hulking dolt Hara, her new lapdog, though Hara was staggering and bloodstained himself.

Sweat broke out on the King's brow. He wrenched his mind from the forest, forced his eyes open. The wraiths had retreated to the cavern walls. They were twining there, whispering, watching him. The Staff seemed to be quivering in his grip and he glanced at it almost fearfully. Its black diamond surface winked at him slyly in the flickering rainbow light.

For the first time since he had made the Staff his own, it had failed to do his will. Somehow Mab had been protected.

Well, no protection would save her a second time. Snarling, the King tightened his grip on the Staff. This decided things. He would make an end to Mab, once and for all, and the other wretches in the forest, too. The wraiths would not like it, would not understand it, but he did not have to explain himself to them!

Confidence swelled in him. What had he been thinking of? He was the Master of the Staff of Tier, and could do anything he willed. Britta's voyage on the *Star of Deltora* had reminded him what it was to feel fear, but all that was in the past. There was nothing to fear any longer.

He felt a tremor in his arm. He felt a sudden pressure, almost as if …

Puzzled, he looked at the Staff again. His heart gave a great, plunging thud. The Staff was leaning, leaning away from him, a little more every moment. He could see it straining against the hand that had gripped it so firmly, and for so long. He could feel the wasted muscles of his arm tensing painfully in the effort to hold it back.

He caught a tiny movement out of the corner of his eye, and looked down. Again his heart plunged in his chest. He stared in shock and disbelief.

A small, amber-colored figure was digging busily in the ground around the Staff's base. It must have been at work for some time because already the hole was broad and deep. Already much of the Staff's base had been uncovered. And, free of the earth that had held it steady, the Staff was tilting—tilting towards the digging creature—as if it was willing, even eager, to stray from the one who called himself its Master.

The King growled deep in his throat, heat rising within him. The amber creature looked up. Its eyes glittered. Its mouth was a small, straight line.

Flame burst from the King's roaring, dripping jaws. A blaze white-hot with rage and dread blasted the hole in the earth like a thunderbolt. But the goozli could move faster than flame. By the time the fire hit the ground, the little clay figure had swarmed more than halfway up the Staff.

It clung there for an instant with fire raging beneath it and the straining fingers that gripped the Staff clamped tight above its head. Then it arched its back and with both its tiny hands, it pulled.

The Staff leaned farther, farther towards the ground. Jerked forward, clinging to his throne with his free hand, the King of Tier bellowed, spitting gobs of fire. Snakes burst from the cavern floor, their fangs dripping venom. Ragged birds of prey swooped, screeching, from above, and giant scorpions swarmed from cracks in the gem-studded walls. The King howled at them all to attack, to kill!

But none of the horrors that he had called into being could touch the goozli. They blundered uselessly around it, savaging one another, while it hung, unharmed, on the black diamond Staff and looked at the King, its eyes now cold as pebbles on a forgotten beach.

The King cried out in dread. "I am the Master of the Staff!" he babbled, as the goozli jumped lightly to the ground, beckoning to the Staff to follow. "You cannot take it from me! It knows my flesh. It knows my name. It cleaves to me alone. Any living soul who tries to take it from me will be slain!"

Any living soul ...

He met the remorseless, inhuman gaze of the little clay doll. His face went blank with terror as at last he understood. But still he clung to his throne. And still he kept hold of the black diamond Staff, though his arm was ablaze with pain. He could not have let his treasure go, even if he had wanted to. The fingers that had gripped it for more than eight long years would never loosen now.

But slowly the Staff tilted away from him. And slowly, as the scorched, crumbling earth gave up its hold, the Staff's base, buried for so long in the island's heart, broke through the ground, into the light.

The wraiths howled. The island shuddered once, and was still. As the Staff began to topple, the King's chilling screams echoed from the dimming walls ...

Then there was a brittle, cracking sound. The screams broke off abruptly. The fighting beasts and the golden throne shivered into dust.

And suddenly all that was left on the cavern floor was the huddled, shrunken body of a man with blood on his lips—a man who had called himself mighty, and thought he would live forever.

In the dimness, the goozli watched, unmoved, as the Staff thudded softly to the ground, taking with it its dead Master's clutching hand. Torn from the lifeless body in the dust, the hand was already shrinking to a claw of dry white bones.

11 - The Lure of the Staff

The sunlight of late afternoon lapped at the cave entrance. Warm fingers of pale gold reached into the shadows and touched the eyelids of the girl lying there. Britta stirred. Ghostly voices were whispering her name. She could hear a soft, dragging sound, coming closer. When it stopped, she opened her eyes.

The goozli was standing beside her, watching her, its head tilted enquiringly, its tiny hands gripping the muddy tip of a long, black Staff.

By the magic of the turtle man the Staff came to me. It knows my flesh. It knows my name …

The words floated dreamily in the mists of Britta's mind as she gazed at the treasure lying in the dust beside her. Ancient, powerful, beautiful, the Staff of Tier shone in the reaching beams of sunlight. Its lure was very strong. Its promises were dazzling. Britta knew that all she had to do to make it her own was to tell it her name, and claim it. Then she would have everything her heart desired, and she would never die.

Dazed with wonder, she sat up. Aching with longing, she put out her hand …

Then she saw the clutch of pale bones that still clung to the Staff's shaft, and a cold sliver of memory pierced the fog in her mind. She saw sunken eyes that did not reflect the light. And in those eyes she saw the madness of a raging will and the darkness of a shriveled soul. Shuddering, she snatched her hand away and put it behind her back.

"No," she mumbled. "No!"

Wailing, the wraiths came rushing from the walls, but did not dare come near. Britta could see them, twining together in the dimness, their ghostly arms stretched out to her, to the Staff.

The goozli took no notice of them. It looked down at the Staff then up at Britta, cocking its head enquiringly once more.

Into Britta's mind swam a picture of the gentle sorcerer Tier, molding amber clay into shapes that moved while the birds of the Two Moons swamp sang around him. She thought of Tier later, betrayed and far from home, fashioning the Staff of Life and Death to wreak his revenge on humankind.

Had Tier meant his revenge to stretch over all eternity? Perhaps he had, in his rage that first day on his new island's shore. But did his spirit want it still?

If it did, would I be here, now? Britta thought.

The goozli was waiting, its small black eyes unblinking.

"The Staff has no Master now," Britta said. "Please do with it what Tier would have wished."

The goozli bowed. And smiled.

When Sky and Jewel came looking for Britta shortly afterward, the cavern was dark and silent. Nothing remained within the great, echoing space but the faint, sour smell of cold ash and the body of the King of Tier lying huddled in the drift of dust that had once been a golden throne.

"Where is she?" Jewel whispered in dread, as she and Sky crept back to the light. "If she had left here, we would have met her on the path."

"She may not have taken the path," said Sky. "She may not have wanted to meet us." Abruptly he turned and began to run back the way they had come.

"Wait! Where are you going?" Jewel shouted after him, but Sky did not answer, and he did not stop.

Britta stood on the glittering shore, wraiths wailing and pleading around her in a coiling gray cloud. The great turtles that dotted the beach had all stretched out their necks to watch as the goozli set the black diamond Staff rolling slowly down towards the sea.

The Staff came to a stop just above a curving line crusted with seaweed and tiny shells. The first wave that broke after that did not reach it. Neither did the second. But when the third wave broke, the warm salt water of the Silver Sea surged eagerly past the line, and the Staff was engulfed in hissing foam.

The wraiths howled. For an instant, the long black shape seemed to writhe. For an instant, the foam bubbled and spat. Then the Staff began to dissolve and melt away. From the sand of the Hungry Isle it had been fashioned, and to that same sand it was returning.

By the time the water ran rippling back to the sea, tumbling a small tangle of white bones with it, the Staff of Tier had gone. All that remained to show where it had been was a shallow pleat in the gleaming sand.

The anguished howling stopped. Time itself seemed to stop.

Britta stood frozen in the sudden silence. Her ears were still ringing, but tormented shades no longer swirled in the mist that hung about her. Instead, she could see human faces—hundreds of human faces—old and young, beautiful and plain, foolish and wise. She could see sailors and traders, travelers and treasure hunters, fishing folk and castaways, a bride and groom in the wedding finery of long ago …

The magic Staff that had enthralled them and held them captive in the world of the living was no more. Their long bondage had ended. Their faces were as serene as the washed sand of the beach. Their eyes, filled with joy and gratitude, were shining like stars. For the last time, Britta felt their soft touch tingling on her skin. Then an icy gale thrilled through her, and they were gone.

Sky burst onto the sand from the dimness of the forest path and stopped, dazzled and gasping. The sky was a dreaming dome of cloudless blue. The sea was like liquid silver in the sunlight. And the shore ... the shore was moving, rippling like water! For an instant Sky blinked in wild confusion. Then he rubbed his streaming eyes and realized what he was seeing.

The turtles were on the move. They were crawling back to the sea, so closely packed together that their huge shells were almost touching. Some were in the shallows already. Most were still making their slow way down the shore. There were only two places on the beach where the tide of moving creatures parted. One was where the landing boat lay drawn up above the high-water mark. The other was where Britta sat, her knees drawn up to her chin, her bent head pillowed on her arms.

Sky's heart gave a sickening thud. He began to run. He was too late, he knew he was too late, but still he ran, dodging and stumbling down to the bare patch of sand where Britta huddled.

"Britta!" he panted as he threw himself down beside her. "Where is it? Where is the Staff?"

"Gone." The voice was very faint.

Bile rose in Sky's throat. This was what he had feared. The moment he saw the turtles leaving the beach as if their task was complete, the moment he saw Britta sitting alone with no wraiths twining around her, he knew what she had done. But still he could not believe it—could not make himself believe it.

"Is it buried in the sand?" he demanded, looking around wildly. "Is it hidden in the forest? Britta, answer me!"

"Not—hidden," the faint voice murmured after a moment. "Gone. Destroyed. The sea …"

Rage swept through Sky—hot rage he had not felt since he was a puny boy in Rithmere, shouting at his mother for gambling away the few coins he had scraped together to pay their rent.

"You had no right!" he spat. "The Staff was a priceless treasure! If you could not face keeping it because of what your cursed father did, why did you not offer it to someone else? Why did you not offer it to *me?* I wanted it—I would have given my soul for it!"

Slowly, wearily Britta raised her head. She saw Sky's lean, familiar face grown sharp and pale. She saw his narrowed eyes glittering like the black sand in the heat of the sun. She saw how the Staff of Tier had cast its spell on him during his time in the cavern, how avidly he had listened to its silent promises of untold wealth and power.

She knew how strong the Staff's lure was. Of

course she did—she had felt it herself. As she stared in misery at the mask of frustrated greed that Sky's face had become, her vision blurred and she seemed to see other faces—Jewel's, Mab's, Hara's, Vashti's, even Healer Kay's—changed and hardened by the same, evil dreams of absolute power.

"That … is why," she whispered. She saw Sky become quite still. She saw his eyes widen in quick, shamed understanding. Then her strength failed her. She bent her head, and said no more.

The days and nights that followed were lost to Britta. She had no sense of time passing, no sense of who was with her, no sense of where she was. Never fully asleep or fully awake, she huddled silently with Mab and Healer Kay in the stern of the landing boat, eating nothing but sipping obediently from a water flask when it was put to her lips.

Sometimes she thought she was lying ill at home, with her mother and Margareth talking softly by her bedside. Sometimes she thought she was sitting by the River Del with Jantsy, when the violets were in bloom. Sometimes she thought she was in her bunk on the *Star of Deltora.*

But never did she think that she was in a boat being rowed steadily away from the Isle of Tier, because where her memories of her time on Tier should have been, there was only darkness.

When Healer Kay stroked her brow and said she was a brave girl, she vaguely wondered why. When Jewel came to tell her not to worry, that all would be well, she barely heard. When Sky crouched beside her, murmuring that he had been ten times a fool, that of course she had been right to destroy the evil, treacherous thing, and that he had told no one what had happened, she merely enjoyed the sound of his husky voice.

Lost in the strange half-world of her shocked, bruised mind she felt no fear as the boat glided on through a wasteland of sea. She felt no pity for the exhaustion of Jewel and Sky, who took most of the burden of the rowing. She felt no admiration for Captain Hara, doggedly plotting their course for Illica by his compass and the stars. She felt no surprise when Vashti took the oars with Kay, so that Jewel and Sky could sleep. She did not think about Mab, who was so silent and so still. She did not notice when the food ran out, and the sips of water she was offered became fewer.

And so it was that she felt no joy when one fine morning a sail appeared on the horizon. She did not notice Hara tearing off his stained white shirt and waving it wildly above his head, or see Jewel holding her gold armband high and twisting it back and forth so it flashed in the sun like a beacon. She barely heard the shouts of amazement as the ship came closer, and was recognized. But when she heard the name *Star of*

Deltora, something stirred in her numb mind and she looked up.

Waving crewmen lined the ship's rail. With them were a sturdy, freckled young woman in blue and a thin young man.

"By all the serpents and little fishes!" Hara bellowed hoarsely. "That girl ... it's Vorn the Boat! And that scrawny fellow must be the lad she ran away with—Olla-Scollbow's son—what was his name—Collin, that's it! I thought they were fish food long ago! What in the nine seas are they doing on the *Star?*"

The world is wide and full of wonders ...

The words floated through Britta's mind like the memory of a dream. For some reason, they made her sad. She let them go.

"More to the point, where is Crow?" Kay muttered.

"At the bottom of the sea, with luck," said Jewel.

Britta stopped trying to pay attention. The light flashing from the sea seemed far too bright. She closed her eyes to shut it out. Excited voices still gabbled around her, but soon they grew fainter, till after a time she could not hear them at all.

12 - Dreaming and Waking

Britta woke as she was being lifted onto the ship, wind whipping about her, spray spattering her face. She did not have the strength to open her eyes, but she could hear people chattering around her.

"Collin and Vorn … on the *Star* all the time!"

"They drugged Crow's rum barrel … Crow and his cronies out like snuffed candles … locked up below … the rest of the crew happy as flying fish …"

"Collin told them that he'd been making the sounds that had scared them in the night … terrible nightmares … crew agreed to come back for us …"

"Will Britta of Del be …?"

"Sshh … deep shock … sorcery, perhaps."

"And Trader Mab? Is she …?"

"Sshh!"

When Britta next stirred, her head and shoulders were propped up on two pillows and a sheet was drawn neatly up to her chin. A faint smell of herbs hung in the air. She could hear soft footsteps and the tiny, familiar creaks of a ship at sea.

Of course! She was no longer in the landing boat, but on the *Star of Deltora.* Thanks to Collin and Vorn, who had caused her so much trouble on Illica, the *Star* had come back to her.

A glorious feeling of safety and peace stole through Britta's body, from the crown of her head to the tips of her toes. She lay quite still, listening to the comforting sounds of her ship, not wanting the moment to end. But then she heard the footsteps again, and curiosity made her open her eyes.

She found that she was not in her own cabin, but in a far larger space filled with that golden dimness created by strong sunlight filtering through thin curtains. Her silk blouse and red skirt hung from a hook on the back of the door. She looked down and saw that she was wearing one of her patched nightdresses. Someone must have undressed her and put her to bed.

And whoever it was must have felt the goozli in her skirt pocket—perhaps looked to see what it was, and wondered why in the nine seas she was carrying a little clay doll about with her. Britta felt a surge of panic, and with the panic came another thought. She raised her hand to the top of her head and felt for the odi shell clip that the goozli had put in her hair the night before the mutiny. It was not there.

"Well, well," a voice said briskly. "So you have decided to join the land of the living, my dear!"

Someone appeared beside the bed and warm fingers were pressed to Britta's wrist. Britta turned her head slightly on the pillows and saw the blunt, pleasant face of Healer Kay. She also saw a little bedside shelf, fixed to the wall. On the shelf, beside a beaker of water, were her comb, notebook, pencil and folded handkerchief. Also the string of false sunrise pearls. Her skirt pockets had been emptied, then. But where was the goozli?

A memory flickered at the edge of Britta's mind, but she could not catch hold of it. It was something about the goozli. Something …

"Your pulse is a little rapid, but I suppose we cannot have everything," said Kay after a moment.

Britta's head felt full of fog. "Kay," she croaked. "In my skirt pocket, did you find …?"

"Do not worry yourself, my dear. All your things are on the shelf here, quite safe. Was there something in particular you wanted?"

"No," Britta said quickly. "I mean—yes! A—a hair clip, Kay. Blue. I was wearing it when …"

"Yes, so you were." Kay's face puckered in concern. "I remember noticing it in the landing boat. But there was nothing in your hair when I put you to bed, Britta. The clip must have fallen out and been lost. What a pity."

"Yes," Britta murmured. She felt hollow inside, but what else was there to say?

"It is nowhere in this cabin, I am sure," Kay said. "If it was, I would surely have found it after all this time."

All this time ...?

Britta licked her lips and found they were dry and cracked. "How long ...?" she managed to ask.

"It has been just over two weeks since you were carried in here, more dead than alive," Kay answered calmly.

"Two weeks!" Britta stared, wide-eyed.

"You are on the sofa in Mab's cabin for now," Kay went on. "It was easier for me to have both my patients in the same place, you see."

She glanced over her shoulder. Following her eyes, Britta saw a wide bunk fixed to the opposite wall. Against the white pillows she could make out the shape of Mab's beaky nose and a thin, trailing plait of faded red hair.

"I hope you do not mind too much," Kay added, a little awkwardly. "It is not as if you will have to speak to Mab. She sleeps most of the time, and even when she stirs she is not up to talking."

Britta was not sure how to reply, so she said nothing. Surely Mab would be the one to object to sharing a cabin with her, not the other way round.

Kay rubbed her nose violently. "Yes, well, enough of that! We have other things to discuss, my dear. You have been very ill, you know, and I must say that your recovery so far is nothing short of a miracle. I doubt it had anything to do with me—I have been working in the dark as far as your treatment is concerned. Now, I do not want to distress you, but it would help me a great deal if you could tell me what happened to you after you left us on the island."

Britta stared at her, puzzled. Surely Healer Kay already knew what had happened—as much as anyone knew, at least, except Sky and Jewel. Why did she want to hear the whole sad tale again?

"Jewel and I went to a bathhouse," she said after a moment. "I traded for the red skirt. Later I went to Scollbow Tower, and Collin—"

"Not Illica, my dear," Kay broke in, a crease appearing between her eyebrows. "Tier! Tier—the Hungry Isle."

"Tier?" The fog swirled in Britta's mind. "I—do not know what you mean. We were in Illica. We set sail for home. The turtles came. There was a mutiny. We were put into the landing boat ..." Her eyelids drooped. She struggled to keep them open.

"Never mind," Kay said quickly. "You are on the mend now, and that is all that matters." Briefly she rested the back of her hand on Britta's forehead.

"You *do* know we are aboard the *Star of Deltora,* Britta?" she asked, in a casual voice.

"Of course," Britta mumbled fretfully. It seemed to her that Kay was being very stupid all of a sudden.

"Then you know you are quite safe, and all is well," said Kay, making a great business of tweaking the bedclothes straight. "The mark on your forehead has faded at last, too, which is another good thing. Now, before you go back to sleep I want you to eat a little soup. I have it here, keeping warm. Just rest quietly while I fetch it."

Rest quietly? Britta almost smiled. What else could she do but rest? She felt as weak as a newborn kitten. She had plainly been very ill, as Kay had said. But what was the matter with her? And why had Kay talked of the Hungry Isle as if ...?"

Kay reappeared at the bedside with a small bowl and a spoon. She pulled up a chair and sat down.

"Kay," Britta began, "please tell me—"

Before she could go on, her mouth had been filled with lentil soup.

"No more talking for you now, my girl," Kay said firmly. "For the next few days you are to pretend you are a goat in a field and do nothing but eat and sleep. After that—we shall see."

When Britta woke next, something warm and heavy was pressed against her feet, and she could hear a rumbling sound like the wheels of a cart rolling over hard ground. Cautiously she opened her eyes. It was night. The rumbling sound was coming from a dark, furry lump at the end of her bed. Someone was sitting in a chair beside her, too—someone whose broad shoulders and shaved head were silhouetted in the soft light of an oil lamp burning somewhere near.

"Jewel," Britta whispered. "What are you doing here?"

Jewel tensed, then turned quickly towards her. "Davvie has a toothache, and Kay has gone to see what she can do for him," she whispered back. "I am to fetch her if she is needed. How are you feeling?"

"Better—better than before, in any case. Is that Black Jack on the end of my bed?"

Jewel nodded. "Kay brought him in—she says she has heard a mouse scuttling round in here."

A mouse? Britta thought of the goozli, and her heart gave a little leap of hope.

"If there *is* a mouse, it is perfectly safe," Jewel went on. "That lazy cat has done nothing so far but make himself comfortable on your bed and drive me mad with his infernal purring. Still, better he purrs than—"

She broke off, clearing her throat noisily. Britta eyed her curiously, wondering what was the matter with her.

There was a short, awkward silence. On the other side of the cabin, Mab made a small, snoring sound, mumbled, and then was still.

"Jewel—" Britta began.

"Sky sends greetings," Jewel said rapidly, at the same moment. "And by the way, do you remember his telling us that he was sure Collin and Vorn were safe? Well, of course he was sure, the wretch! He had just discovered them hiding in the cargo hold! Whatever he promised them, can you believe he did not tell us?"

She took a breath and hurried on. "It seems they hid the boat they stole on the blind side of the island, to leave a false trail, then came back and crept aboard the *Star*. They are married now—Hara performed the ceremony—ship's captains can do that at sea, of course. Collin is mad to see you. He and Vorn want to thank you, he says."

"From what I have heard, I should be thanking them," Britta said. "Did they really manage to drug Crow, Bolt and the others?"

Jewel leaned forward, for the first time looking more like her normal self. "They did," she whispered, her eyes sparkling. "And you will never guess what they used to do it!"

Britta shrugged. "Kay's supplies—"

Jewel shook her head. "Bolt had taken over Kay's cabin, so they did not dare go there. No—they found the sleeping potion in another cabin—Vashti's!"

She grinned at the expression on Britta's face. "They were searching for weapons, of course, but then they found this little bottle hidden away among some petticoats, and Vorn knew what it was, by its smell. The bottle was not quite full, but there was still enough of the mixture left to put Crow and his louts out of action for a good long time. It is powerful stuff,

Vorn says."

"Very powerful, in my experience," Britta said dryly.

"Yes, there is no longer any mystery about who drugged your water in Two Moons, little nodnap," Jewel agreed. "Vashti denies it, of course, but she looked so guilty when Vorn gave the bottle back to her that Sky and I are sure she was the culprit. We will never be able to prove it, but at least we know."

"Yes, that is one mystery solved, at least." Britta tried to smile.

"And here is another," Jewel went on. "Collin *did* take that sunrise pearl from Scollbow Tower. When I told him that you had been accused of stealing it, he was very shocked. That is the other reason he wants to see you. But Kay insists you are to be kept quiet."

She looked at Britta with sudden attention, and grimaced. "And by the serpent's tongue, Kay would skin me alive if she saw your face now! I have tired you by talking too much."

"No!" Britta stretched out her hand impulsively. "It is so good to see you, Jewel! And I *need* to talk. I have so many questions ..." She paused, feeling strangely embarrassed, then gathered up her courage and plunged on. "There seem to be things I cannot remember. You must tell me—"

"I am not supposed to talk to you about all that," Jewel broke in, shaking her head. "Kay gave me strict orders—"

"Please!" Britta begged. "I must know. Did I dream it, or did Kay say we landed on—on the Hungry Isle?"

Jewel made a small, helpless sound. "So you really remember nothing at all, Britta?" she muttered. "About the cavern, and the Staff of Tier? About—your father?"

Britta's head began to swim. The bed seemed to be quaking beneath her. She gripped the sheet with both hands as if to hold herself still. Pictures were flashing before her eyes. A black beach dotted with turtles. A cavern mouth filled with starry mist. Mab screaming, crumpling to the ground …

Jewel was whispering urgently but Britta could not answer. Her teeth were chattering. She could not make them stop. She heard a muttered curse. She heard the chair clatter as Jewel jumped up and ran.

Then she heard a tiny click from somewhere beside her head, and the next moment something was scuttling across the sheet, onto her straining hands. Britta blinked at it, a strangled cry dying in her throat. The terrifying pictures faded.

Balanced on her knuckles, its mouth curved into a worried little smile, was the goozli.

13 - Questions and Answers

Black Jack raised his head. He stared at the goozli with sleepy golden eyes, then yawned and settled down again. "I thought I had lost you, goozli," Britta whispered. The goozli bounced on her hands and shook its head reproachfully.

"Yes, I should have known you would not let yourself be left behind," Britta said. "And of course you could not show yourself to me while Kay was—"

She broke off as the goozli cocked its head and put its finger to its lips. An instant later she heard hurrying footsteps and Kay's scolding mutter, growing louder.

The goozli darted to the side of the sofa, swung itself under the shelf jutting from the wall there, and vanished. Britta heard another little click. And suddenly she was remembering the model of the *Star of Deltora* in Captain Gripp's cottage. Suddenly she was a child again, kneeling beside the model, playing one of her games. She was hiding a tiny, rolled-up "treasure map' in what she called "the secret safe," a small cavity in the wall below a shelf in the chief trader's cabin.

Gripp had told her that the safe was a secret. Dare Larsett had made it himself, and no one else but Gripp and Britta knew of it. When its door flap was shut it looked just like part of the wall, and who would think to look under an awkward shelf beside a sofa anyway? Perhaps even Mab did not know it was there. The goozli had found the perfect hiding place.

There was no time to think any more. Kay was hurrying through the doorway with Jewel behind her.

"I am all right," Britta protested, as Kay took her pulse, looking searchingly into her face. "Truly, Kay!"

"Britta, I am so sorry," Jewel whispered. "I did not think—"

"I warned you, Jewel of Broome!" Kay said grimly, releasing Britta's wrist at last. "As it happens, you were lucky—there seems to be no great harm done. But Britta's mind needs rest, and—"

"Kay!" Britta cut in. "Healer Kay, please listen to me!"

She was glad to see Kay look surprised at the strength in her voice. Determined to go on as she had begun, Britta took a deep breath.

"I know that you have been trying to protect me, Kay, and I am grateful. But I cannot rest knowing that there is a gaping hole in my memory. I must be told what I cannot remember for myself."

"I am sure that much of your memory will return in time, Britta," Kay said. "You must be patient and wait—"

"I cannot wait!" Britta burst out, forgetting to keep her voice down. "You do not understand!"

Her throat closed, but she swallowed furiously and forced herself to go on. "I gather you all know about my father now, and I—I imagine that you all feel very differently about me as a result."

She heard Jewel make a small, protesting sound, but did not look round.

"The news will spread very fast in Del, once we land," she went on, keeping her voice as steady as she could. "I must know what happened on the Hungry Isle before then. I must have time to prepare myself for whatever may be in store for me and—and for my mother and sister."

She swallowed hard again and made herself turn to Kay. The healer's gray eyes were filled with pity.

"Yes, I see," Kay said quietly. "I had not thought of it that way, Britta, but of course you are right." She sighed and ran her fingers through her hair. "It will be as you wish. Jewel will tell you what you need to know. I will be on hand if you need me."

So at last Britta heard the story of what had happened on the Isle of Tier—as much as Jewel knew, at least. Mostly it was as if Jewel was telling her a tale that had happened to someone else. Only sometimes did flashes of memory come to her. They were disturbing, but less horrifying than they had been before because now she understood what they meant.

Jewel told her story flatly, with as little detail as possible. But still it was a tale that was very hard for Britta to hear, for at its heart were her father's wickedness, her father's broken bargain and her father's death. She heard the last of it with a bowed head. Her chest and throat were aching. It would have been a relief to cry, but as usual her eyes were dry.

Now she understood why Jewel had at first seemed uneasy with her. How did you treat a sick, troubled friend whose lies had put you in peril, but who had saved you by somehow causing the death of her own father?

And the odd things Kay had said about sharing Mab's cabin now made sense. Kay thought Britta must hate Mab for using her as bait for the King of Tier.

Mab's plan was one of the few things Britta now remembered clearly. The scene in front of the cavern had come back to her vividly as Jewel described watching her walk towards the starry mist with Mab. She remembered the scalding sense of betrayal she had felt at the time. She felt it still, but not so keenly. It was as if the things that had happened afterward had drained away much of its power to hurt.

Things that had happened afterward ... Britta turned her head to look at the old woman lying so still in the bunk on the other side of the cabin. According to Jewel, Mab had been struck down because of her plan—had almost paid for it with her life.

Something fluttered in the darkness at the edge of Britta's mind. She tried to drag it into the open, and sighed in frustration when it would not come.

She felt a hand on her shoulder. "Mab would not be alive now if it were not for you, Britta," Jewel said in a low voice. "None of us would. How you managed to get the Staff away from your father no one will ever know, unless the memory comes back to you in time. But somehow you did it—you did what you had to do. You saved us, and because the Staff fell to dust with your father's death, you also put an end to the Hungry Isle for good. To anyone of sense, nothing else should matter. In Broome you will be hailed as a hero, I promise you!"

"Del is not Broome, I fear," Britta said with a rueful smile. But she reached up and squeezed Jewel's hand gratefully. As she did, she noticed the golden armband gleaming in the dim light and another flicker of memory came to her.

"Your armband is a weapon!" she murmured. "You fought with it in the forest!"

"There, you see? You are remembering more all the time!" Jewel glanced down at the armband and shrugged. "Yes, the kish is useful when no other weapon is at hand. It is a pity that so many people saw me using it, though. It is supposed to be secret. I am sure that most of you will keep quiet about it, but I doubt that Vashti will."

Britta sighed. She doubted it too. She was sure that Vashti would not keep quiet about anything.

Despite Kay's fears, that night marked the beginning of Britta's real recovery—in one way, at least. She could feel herself growing stronger every day, but her memories of the Hungry Isle were still just a few flickering pictures that had added little to what Jewel had told her. The rest was darkness.

Increasingly she had the nagging feeling that something important, something very important, was hidden in that darkness. But the more she strained to recall it, the thicker the darkness seemed to become, and at last she made herself stop trying.

Soon she was well enough to leave her bed, and even take short walks on deck, holding Jewel's arm.

These walks were both a joy and a depressing reminder of what was to come. The glorious feeling of the fresh breeze on her face and the sight of the *Star*'s sails white against the clear blue sky filled her with deep happiness. The avid stares of the crew and her glimpses of Vashti turning quickly away, drawing in her skirts as if to avoid infection, were hard to bear.

"Take no notice," Jewel advised. "You know what Vashti is. And you cannot blame the men for being curious about you. Officially they have been told very little, but they seem to know everything all the same. At least they do not fear you any longer—that is the main thing."

The walks made Britta feel stifled in Mab's dim, hushed cabin, and at Kay's suggestion she began to spend the daylight hours sitting in the healer's cabin next door. There she could have the curtains drawn back to let in the sun. She could also talk to her visitors without having to whisper.

It was Sky she really longed to see, but Captain Hara, shorthanded because Crow and his henchmen were locked up below, was keeping Sky so busy that it was a long time before she was to have her wish.

In the meantime, there was Jewel and, of course, Collin of Illica. Collin came, bubbling over with thanks and bursting with pride about the overthrow of the mutiny.

"It was all Vorn's idea," he told Britta. "When you and the others were put overboard I thought we were doomed. But Sky had told us that the boy Davvie and Grubb the cook were to be trusted, so Vorn decided we should show ourselves to them and ask them to help us drug Crow's rum. The plan worked to a marvel. Vorn is always right."

As he was leaving, he said he was very sorry that his parents had taken Britta's sunrise pearl. "I wish I could give you ours to replace it," he added, nodding earnestly. "But, as Vorn says, it is all we have, and we will need it to buy tools and such when we get to Del.

We are going to build and repair boats, you know. That is Vorn's plan."

He was so happy that Britta could only nod and force a smile. But she was glad to see him go. The thought of her lost pearl made her feel ill.

Captain Hara's visit, some days later, was more surprising and very much shorter. He did not even come into the cabin, just loomed in the doorway, regarding Britta without a flicker of a smile. His neck was still bruised, but otherwise he looked as fit as ever.

"I came to tell you something," he said abruptly. "It's been on my mind, and now you know what Mab was up to, there's no reason for me to keep quiet about it any longer."

Seeing him standing there, burly and serious, made something click in Britta's mind.

"It was *you* who attacked me and locked me up in Del that night, Captain Hara!" she burst out.

The corner of Hara's mouth tightened in surprise, and he nodded.

"I suspected everyone else, but never *you*—not until this moment," Britta went on. "But—but why did you do it? Were you trying to stop Mab from—?"

"Hardly," Hara growled. "I was following Mab's orders—or thought I was. You, Vashti, Jewel and Sky had equal scores, and at that time we all thought there could be three finalists only. You had to be one of them. The easiest way to be sure of that was to put one of the others out of the way. Vashti's parents would have raised an almighty stink if anything happened to her. Jewel would have put up too much of a fight. So—"

Light broke. Britta almost laughed. "You took me for Sky!" she exclaimed. "Because I'd disguised myself in old clothes like his, and let my hair hang loose! You thought you were pushing *Sky* into that cellar!"

"That's it," Hara said. "It was dark, and from behind you looked … Anyhow, I thought all was well, and I told Mab so. Then, blow me down, Sky turned up at the Traders Hall with Jewel, and there was no sign of you."

He shook his head in disgust. "Mab was beside herself! I caught on to what must have happened, and went back for you. By all the serpents and little fishes, I've never run so fast! For a while there I thought the whole plan had run aground."

"It might have been better for all of us if it had," Britta could not help saying. "But thank you for telling me."

Hara shrugged. "If the wind stays fair we'll be in Del in a couple of days. I wanted you to know before we landed and the hullabaloo began. Put in a complaint to the Trust, if you like—it might get you some sympathy. I won't have a future with the Rosalyn fleet after this, anyway. And without Mab as the Trader I don't want one. I can't see myself serving under Vashti, even if she'd have me."

He gave Britta a curt nod, and left her.

14 - Two Days to Del

Two days to Del! The news had stunned Britta more than anything else Hara had said. She felt panic-stricken. Her illness and the long, slow weeks of her recovery had made her lose all track of time. Why had Kay and Jewel not warned her that the voyage was so nearly over?

Because they did not want you to fret and worry, the voice of reason told her. *Because they know you have made some sort of plan for your family, and are as well prepared as you can be.*

Yes, Britta thought dismally. But I had so hoped—

A tap on the door made her jump.

"Come in," she called, and her heart gave a strange little lurch as Sky of Rithmere slouched into the cabin, bringing with him the smell of the sea.

"Sky!" she cried, half rising from her chair.

Sky seemed not to see her outstretched hand. He

perched on the edge of Kay's bunk and looked around the cabin.

"So, Britta—how are you feeling?" he asked, as casually as if they had seen each other just the day before.

Plainly he had not missed her at all. Grateful that she had not betrayed herself by saying something stupid, Britta let irritation swamp her disappointment.

"In two days, everyone in Del will know I am Dare Larsett's daughter," she snapped. "My mother and sister will be disgraced along with me. We will have to leave the city and start again—in Broome, if I can persuade Mother to agree. Soon I will lose the *Star of Deltora*—to Vashti! I am so weak that I cannot totter the length of the deck without a rest, and I have a black hole in my memory. How do you *think* I feel?"

"Not so well?" Sky murmured.

Britta snorted with angry laughter. "Not so well. And you?"

Sky's thin lips twisted into a crooked smile. "Things could be better. I lost the treasures from Bar-Enoch's cave—they must have fallen from my pocket during the fight in the forest. Just my luck. You lost the odi shell clip, too, I hear, and Crow and his louts smashed Jewel's trade from Two Moons, so we are all returning to Del empty-handed."

Britta bit her lip. Jewel had said nothing about losing her trade. But that was typical of Jewel.

"Still, at least I have had some ocean sailing

experience now," Sky said with a shrug. "Later I might be able to get work as a deckhand on some ship or other, if the captain is not too choosy."

"Hara seems to think well of you," Britta replied coolly. "Perhaps you could sign on with him, wherever he goes after this."

"Perhaps."

There was a short silence. Britta pressed her lips together, determined not to be the one to break it.

"Do you really remember very little of Tier, Britta?" Sky asked abruptly, in quite a different tone.

"Very little." Britta sighed, forgetting for the moment to keep her cool mask in place. "Kay says it is a blessing, but I keep thinking that among all the other things I have forgotten there is something very important. It is driving me mad!"

Sky hesitated, then seemed to come to a decision.

"I think I can help," he said. "I confess I was tempted not to tell you—to let the whole thing go, or at least to leave out the part concerning me. But perhaps if I grit my teeth and tell it all ..."

Flashing pictures of white foam boiling on black sand came to Britta as she listened to Sky's story of what had happened between them on the shore of the Hungry Isle. She was shivering by the time he fell silent.

"This explains some things I did not understand about Jewel's story," she said in a low voice. "I knew the Staff would not have fallen to dust just because

Father died. And I could not think why I went to the shore with the wraiths, or why they were released from the island only then. But Jewel seemed to have no doubt—"

"I did not tell anyone what you did—even Jewel," Sky broke in. "I did not want the word to spread. Many people would condemn you for destroying the Staff—as I did, before I came to my senses. I squirm when I think how I raged at you."

He grimaced, staring down at his hands. "This can go down in history as the first time I ever felt ashamed of anything. Shame and guilt have always seemed a waste of energy to me."

Very moved, Britta touched his arm. She felt the muscles tense beneath the thin fabric of his sleeve.

Sky looked up. "Sadly, my confession was wasted, it seems. I gather that none of this has helped to bring back the memory that has been troubling you."

"I am afraid not," Britta admitted reluctantly. "The feeling still nags at me. I have begun to think that it is something only I know, that no one else can tell me. But thank you for what you said, Sky. It must have been hard."

"The hardest thing I have ever done," said Sky. "And that includes fighting savage orchids with nothing but my belt and one of Jewel's earrings."

That night, Mab was very restless. Kay tried in vain to

soothe her, and at last padded over to Britta.

"Mab is keeping you awake, my dear, and you need your rest," she whispered. "I am going to ask Jewel to come and help you back to your old cabin. You are well enough for that now, and Jewel can keep an eye on you for me."

She hurried out. Mab mumbled and moaned. There was a tiny click, and the next moment the goozli was bouncing on the sheet beside Britta's cheek.

"Did you hear, goozli?" Britta whispered. "I am going back to my old cabin. Stay hidden, but be sure to keep track of me! We land in two days."

The goozli frowned and tapped its tiny foot.

"Yes, of course you know what to do." Britta sighed. "I wish I did, goozli! Jewel keeps telling me things will be easier to manage than I think, but oh, if only Mab would get well!"

The goozli tilted its head enquiringly.

"Mab would speak for me to the Rosalyn Trust Committee. But even more important than that—I have to get my mother and sister out of Del quickly and quietly, and Mab has the power and gold to arrange it. If she was well, she would surely agree to help—she owes me something for what she did. But as things are …"

She sighed again, and glanced over at Mab's bunk, at the muttering old woman lying there. She thought of Maarie and Margareth, peacefully sleeping above the shop with no idea of the storm that was about to break over their heads. She thought of Jantsy—of how it would feel to part with Jantsy again so soon, and this time, perhaps, forever. She could not imagine it.

"Jantsy will do all he can for us," she murmured, swallowing the lump that had risen in her throat. "Captain Gripp will, too. Neither of them is rich, but perhaps between them they can raise enough to buy a horse and cart. The stock in the shop will go a little way towards paying them back—we will just have to owe them the rest. And if I can persuade Mother to go to Broome, Jewel will lead us. We would be very welcome in Broome, Jewel says. No one will despise us there ..."

Her voice trailed off as she imagined her mother coping with a move to a place that she would see as foreign, savage and wild. Kind, even-tempered Margareth would be happy anywhere, but Maarie ...

For the third time Britta sighed. "It is not much of a plan, is it, goozli?" she said ruefully. "But it is all I have."

The goozli smiled and tapped the side of its tiny nose. Then, as Kay's footsteps sounded outside, it sprang back into hiding, leaving Britta to wonder what the smile had meant.

Two days quickly became one. The *Star* buzzed with activity as the crew scrubbed, polished and stowed, preparing for the landing the following morning.

Sitting in a quiet corner on deck, watching the sun set and trying to keep out of the way, Britta reflected that time had a way of flying just when you wished it would slow to a crawl.

"Vashti can hardly wait to land," Jewel had commented sourly the night before, when she returned from dinner. "She is plainly bursting with the tale she has to tell. Ah, if only I had thought to push her out of the landing boat! Then we could tell any story we liked to the Trust Committee. Mab is too ill to speak, and Hara would not give us away. He has too much to lose himself."

"We would have to bribe the whole crew to silence if we were to get away with a false story, with Vashti or without her," Britta had replied dryly.

And of course the ship's log will tell much of what happened, Britta thought now, letting her notebook fall onto her lap. Hara is loyal to Mab, certainly, but surely he would not tell lies in the log—even to protect her and save his own reputation.

Or would he? A mere five years as captain of the *Star of Deltora* had been enough to bind Hara so closely to Mab that he had been willing to risk his life and his career for her.

So here is another poor fool hypnotized by Mab! Another pet dog who has allowed himself to be used in return for crumbs dropped from the Trader Rosalyn's table!

Britta stiffened as the harsh whisper pierced her thoughts like the hiss of a snake. Her heart thudding painfully, she stood up and began to pace the deck, her notebook gripped tightly in her hand.

She wanted to remember all that she had forgotten, she really did! But if only the memories would come back to her quietly and in order, instead of in these sudden flashes that took her by surprise. She focused on the chilling voice, hoping that more of the scene in the cavern of the Staff would come to her. But as usual nothing happened.

She turned as Davvie came panting up to her with Black Jack at his heels.

"Sky says to tell you that Healer Kay asked Grubb to send a proper dinner to the chief trader's cabin tonight, instead of just broth," Davvie whispered. "Kay didn't say nothing, but Sky thinks it means that Trader Mab has woken up!"

Britta caught her breath. She remembered the goozli smiling and tapping the side of its nose when she wished that Mab would get well. Was this just chance, or—?

Or had she failed yet again to understand the extent of the goozli's power? Did the goozli have some fragment of the life-giving magic of the turtle man Tier—some power to heal? Britta's own recovery had been a miracle, according to Healer Kay. Perhaps the goozli had roused her! And now it had worked the same miracle for Mab ... crept to Mab's bunk in the night while Kay was drowsing, and managed to do what it knew Britta wanted.

As Davvie ran cheerfully away, the cat stalking after him, Britta turned and moved as fast as she could to the stern.

Her heart was filled with hope as she made her way down to the chief trader's cabin. Hope swelled as through the door she clearly heard Mab's voice raised in complaint, and Kay's voice calmly replying. But when she knocked, complete silence fell and the door did not open.

She knocked again. "Mab," she called softly. "Mab, it is Britta! Please may I talk to you?"

She heard voices muttering and pressed her ear to the door.

"Send her away!" she distinctly heard Mab say. "Tell her I am far too ill to see anyone! Tell her I am dying! Curse you, Kay, where is your loyalty?"

There was a moment's silence, then the door opened a crack and Kay peered out, her face red with anger.

"I am sorry, Britta," she said stiffly. "Mab cannot speak to anyone. You had better run along."

The door closed. Her dashed hopes falling like cold rain around her, Britta crept away.

At first she felt merely stunned and unhappy. By the time she reached her own cabin she was furious with herself. What a fool she had been to think that Mab would help her! Mab was a cunning, ruthless woman. Of course, the moment she awoke she must have begun thinking about the best way to protect herself from any claim that she had deliberately sought out the Hungry Isle. And of course the first thing she would decide was that she must cut herself off completely from any contact with the daughter of Dare Larsett. So, to save herself, she had cast Britta adrift.

Still, I am no worse off now than I was before Davvie gave me Sky's message, Britta told herself. *I did not have Mab's help then, and I do not have it now. I still have my plan, for what it is worth. And I will not tell Jewel about this, or she will go storming to Mab's cabin and cause a fuss. That would do me no good and might do Jewel a lot of harm.*

She kept her resolve all through the evening, and even managed to smile at Jewel's wicked imitation of Collin praising Vorn to the skies all through dinner. But her thoughts were bitter as she lay in her bunk later, imagining the goozli faithfully continuing to strengthen Mab, in preparation for the day to come.

15 - The Ceremony

As the *Star of Deltora* surged into Del harbor the following morning, it seemed to Britta that the night had passed in the blink of an eye. She stood at the prow with Jewel, watching the familiar shore draw nearer, and the same dreamlike feeling that had gripped her on the outward journey took hold of her again.

Was it possible that the voyage had ended? That soon she would be leaving the *Star* for good? That, except perhaps for Jewel, the people she had seen every day for months would soon be going their separate ways and out of her life?

She tried to make herself believe it. This was no dream. It was really happening, and she had to pull herself together. She would need all her wits about her to cope with what was to come. She had to bargain—with Trader Sorrel and the rest of the Trust Committee, who would know that she had deceived them, and with her mother, whose new life she had smashed.

Part of the strangeness she felt was because she had put on her old Del clothes—the sober blue skirt and the white shirt the goozli had mended. The garments were not as tight as they had been before, because she had lost weight during her illness, but they still made her feel suffocated. And after weeks of freedom, her hair was again twisted into a tight knot at the nape of her neck and secured by the hard, hated hairpins.

"My mother will be shocked enough by what has happened," she had said, when Jewel eyed her in surprise. "If I go to her dressed in scarlet silk, with my hair falling about my ears, it will make everything ten times worse."

She knew she was right about that, but there was no doubt that putting on the uniform of her past life had been like creeping back into a shell that no longer fit her. She knew, as well, that she looked like a poor, pale copy of Vashti, who was standing as far from her as was possible, confident, blooming and exquisitely neat

At least, Britta thought grimly, *Vashti will be disappointed in one thing. She still thinks Mab is dying, and that it will not be long before Vashti the Rosalyn Apprentice becomes Vashti the Trader Rosalyn. In fact, she will be under the thumb of that treacherous, power-mad old woman for some time yet. I wish her well of it!*

"A crowd is gathering on the dock," Jewel said, squinting into the distance. "Sorrel is there—right at the front."

She shook her head with a frown. "The news of our arrival must be spreading. More people are appearing every moment. Britta, there is no point in your going through the first part of this. You will have to attend the Apprentice ceremony at sunset—even Sky will have to do that, Hara says—but you should go below and keep out of the way till then, or at least until Sorrel sends for you."

Britta hesitated, then nodded. Her impulse was to stand and face the outcry to come with what dignity she could muster, but her sense told her to conserve her strength. Her real battle would come later.

So as the *Star of Deltora* docked, as the first, startling news was given and the expected tumult began, Britta waited below, out of sight. Her mind a blank, she sat with folded hands in her old place at the writing table. She had closed the porthole curtain, but the cabin door was gaping wide, propped open by her bundle of possessions. She wanted to be able to hear Sorrel's messenger approaching. She could not bear to be surprised by a knock on the door.

Feet tramped on the deck above her head. Voices were raised in shock, dismay and anger. Britta did not even try to hear what was being said—she knew.

Her sense of time began to blur as she sat there, the sun strengthening behind the porthole curtain, but at last she became aware that the sounds on the deck were growing less. Her tension rose. When she heard a little scuffle in the doorway her stomach gave a sickening jolt. But it was only the goozli, pattering towards her, jumping onto her outstretched hand and springing onto the tabletop, looking very pleased with itself.

"Goozli, you found me!" Britta exclaimed in relief. The little creature nodded patiently, plainly wondering if she would ever learn to trust it.

"I do trust you," Britta said. "I was only worried because you took so long to come to me. But I daresay you had to wait till there were fewer people about."

The goozli bowed and tapped the side of its nose. Then it stiffened, listening.

Someone was running towards the cabin. Quickly Britta unbuttoned her pocket and held it open. She was buttoning it up again, with the goozli safely inside, when Davvie appeared in the doorway, his eyes wide with fright.

"You—you're to come now, Britta," he whispered. "They're doing the 'prentice ceremony now, instead of later, an' you're wanted." He gulped. "Sky says—Sky says that whatever they say to you, you've got to keep remembering that—that you're you, an' not your father."

Anxiously he looked up at her, worried that

his message made no sense, but Britta nodded and managed a smile.

The dreamlike feeling crept over her again as she followed Davvie along the passage and up to the deck. She could hear the murmuring of a large crowd on the dock, the splash of water, and the soft creaking of the moored ship. The sun was very warm and bright. The salty air was heavy with the familiar harbor smells of spices, tar, fried fish and baked sweet potatoes.

Britta felt dizzy, and for a terrible moment she thought she might faint. She pressed her fingers to the goozli nestled in her pocket, steadied herself, and moved on after Davvie.

A group of people stood waiting in the stern, the Rosalyn flag fluttering gently behind them. In the center was Trader Sorrel. He was looking straight ahead, his silver hair gleaming, his face very grave. On either side of him were some men and women Britta had never seen before—other members of the Rosalyn Trust Committee, no doubt.

Davvie muttered something she did not catch and backed away, leaving her alone. It did not matter. She knew what she had to do. Vashti, Sky and Jewel were standing in a line before the Committee. She had to join them.

She moved stiffly forward, placing her feet very carefully, keeping her back straight. She could feel many eyes upon her. The other members of the Trust Committee turned their heads to stare at her, but Sorrel still looked straight ahead as if he did not know she was there.

As she stepped into line beside Jewel, Britta saw dimly that Captain Hara was standing by the ship's rail, near some other people who were sitting on chairs that must have been brought up from below. A finely dressed couple perched bolt upright on the first two chairs, looking outraged. Beside them lounged a very tall, broad-shouldered woman whose shaved, painted head proclaimed her to be a woman of Broome.

On the very edge of the fourth chair crouched a shrunken, gray-faced old man with a bushy white beard. Confused as she was, it took a moment for Britta to realize that the pathetic, bowed figure was Captain Gripp. As she met Gripp's eyes and saw the love and misery there, her heart turned over.

Someone handed Sorrel a roll of parchment. He unrolled it, cleared his throat and began to read aloud, his voice flat and colorless.

"We, the members of the Trust Committee, are gathered here to appoint the Trader Rosalyn Apprentice, in the presence of the finalists and their sponsors, and of Mab, the Trader Rosalyn ..."

His voice trailed off. He rolled up the parchment again and passed it to the elegant woman standing beside him.

"The written speech was prepared before certain matters became known, and is now out of date," he said, again staring straight ahead. "I will have to speak without it. To correct my previous statement: first, the sponsors of only three of the finalists are present. Captain Hara has explained why this is so."

His bunchy cheeks became rather pink. "During the voyage, it was discovered that the finalist Sky of Rithmere does not qualify for the contest, by the rules of the Rosalyn Trust. I ask him to stand aside, but not to leave this place until he is told he may."

"Disgraceful!" someone hissed as Sky left the line of finalists and moved, with the suggestion of a swagger, to stand just out of Britta's sight.

"Secondly," Sorrel continued, his voice trembling very slightly, "Mab, the Trader Rosalyn, is not present at this ceremony. She is not even aware that it is taking place. On the Isle of Tier, where her boat was forced to land after the mutiny of which we have all heard, she was attacked by Dare Larsett and as a result is gravely ill."

"That is not true!" Jewel burst out. "Mab was ill before we even reached Tier! And—"

"Silence!" Sorrel thundered. "We have heard Captain Hara's report. We require no other."

Britta turned to look at Hara. His bearded face was quite expressionless.

So, she thought numbly, Hara is going to cover up for Mab. No doubt they decided between them last night that if she did not appear at the ceremony, she would not have to answer any awkward questions.

The tall woman who was plainly Jewel's sponsor

shifted in her chair. "If there is a disagreement, surely the matter should be discussed," she remarked to no one in particular.

"With respect, Erin of Broome, I disagree," Vashti's father said smoothly. "You arrived at the dock only minutes ago, so you may not realize how grave our dear Mab's condition is. Time may be very short. That is why it was decided to hold this ceremony as soon as possible, instead of at the traditional time of sunset."

"We had no choice," the elegant woman beside Sorrel added, twisting the roll of parchment in her shaking hands. "It is vital that the Apprentice is named before … before any sad event occurs." Her eyes suddenly filled with tears.

Sorrel went on doggedly, though his voice was still not quite steady. "Because the Trader Rosalyn cannot be with us, the Committee has no choice but to base its decision solely on the value of the goods brought back to Del by each finalist."

He took a card from his pocket and glanced at it. "Vashti, daughter of Irma and Loy of Del, used the ten gold coins that had been given to each finalist to buy a dozen small jade vases. The jade is only of medium quality, but the vases are attractive and we believe they would sell in Del for two golds each. Vashti's trade is therefore valued at twenty-four gold coins."

The other Trust Committee members clapped without much enthusiasm.

"We did not land in Maris, you see," Vashti said breathlessly, "and we had less than a day in Two Moons. I am sure that I would have done very much better if I had been able to follow my trading plan, and—"

"I daresay," Sorrel cut in. "In any case, Vashti, you were fortunate in that your goods were stored in the cargo hold, where I understand the mutineers did not go. Jewel of Broome, on the other hand, had purchased in Two Moons an inlaid music box—"

"I had planned to trade it in Illica," Jewel said. "But—"

"But you did not have the opportunity," finished Sorrel, giving her a hard stare. Clearly he had heard of Jewel's trouble in Illica, but for the sake of the dignity of the Rosalyn Trust he was not going to speak of it in public.

Britta looked quickly over her shoulder to exchange glances with Sky, but discovered that he had vanished. Dully she wondered if he had already slipped off the ship, despite the order to stay on board. Sky had a way of easing himself out of trouble.

"Unfortunately," Sorrel was continuing, "Jewel of Broome kept the music box in her cabin, where it was found by the mutineers and wantonly smashed. As it is, it is worth nothing, and the few trampled fragments that remain are not enough for us even to guess at its previous value."

The elegant woman beside him sighed—more because of the destruction of a beautiful thing, Britta thought, than because she had any sympathy for Jewel.

"And it seems that the remaining finalist, Britta of Del, has brought back nothing at all," Sorrel went on, still looking straight ahead. "Is that correct, Britta?"

He had chosen not to mention Britta's father, or her false entry in the contest. Britta knew that she should be grateful for that. But she could see in Sorrel's eyes, and the eyes of every other person on deck, that everything was known. In the end, she and Captain Gripp would both pay heavily for their deceit.

"That is correct," she made herself say. "My only trade was lost in the Two Moons swamplands."

"And what in the nine seas was she doing *there*, I would like to know?" Vashti's mother hissed, in a piercing whisper that everyone could hear.

"Under the circumstances, therefore," Sorrel said, "the clear and only possible winner of the Rosalyn Apprentice contest is—"

"What is the meaning of this?"

The voice was loud, familiar and furiously angry. Everyone jumped. The people on the dock craned forward.

Supported on one side by Healer Kay and on the other by Sky of Rithmere, Trader Mab was hobbling rapidly towards Sorrel, her red hair flaming in the sun, her eyes spitting fire.

16 - Mab

The crowd on the dock roared, Jewel yelled, and the Trust Committee members froze. The sponsors sprang to their feet. Captain Hara cursed in amazement. Vashti clapped her hand to her mouth to muffle a little scream of shock. For an instant, Sorrel's face was a picture of almost comical amazement. Then he went bright red, and tears of joy sprang into his eyes.

"Mab!" he shouted, all dignity forgotten. "By all the wonders—"

"Why was I not told the ceremony had been put forward?" Mab demanded. She jerked her head at Sky. "If it had not been for this rascal here, Kay and I would never have known! Well, Sorrel? Don't stand blubbering there! Explain yourself!"

Sorrel gaped at her, tears still running down his fiery cheeks.

"We thought you were dying!" roared Jewel's sponsor, who was clearly enjoying herself thoroughly.

Mab turned and glared at Hara.

"Kay said last night that you were too ill to see me," Hara said with a shrug. "This morning, just before we docked, I was told that you could have no visitors and that I should tell the Committee members all they needed to know."

"All Mab *wanted* them to know," Jewel muttered, a little too loudly.

"Curse you, Hara, that did not mean I planned to miss the Apprentice Ceremony!" Mab thundered. "By the heavens, who knows what a muck of it these fools would have made if I had not arrived in time!"

The Committee members exchanged outraged glances. Sorrel's cheeks darkened to dull scarlet.

"I fail to see how we could have made a so-called 'muck of it,' Mab," he said stiffly. "Only one finalist brought traded items of any value back to Del."

"Indeed?" Mab regarded him scathingly. "Then I gather you think that seven lives—one of them mine, I might remind you—have no value? What of a fully equipped landing boat, then?"

Shocked gratitude swept through Britta in a great, warm flood, almost knocking her off her feet. With shame mingled with relief she felt Jewel's arm wrap around her, holding her steady.

Sorrel shied like a startled horse. He darted a glance at Britta, and cleared his throat.

"We had not considered your escape from the Hungry Isle as being a matter of trade," he began carefully. "That is, we understand that by some means Britta of Del made the escape possible—"

"The girl deserves no credit for that!" Vashti's father broke in angrily. "They would not have been on Tier in the first place if it had not been for her! By the heavens, man, she is the daughter of Dare Larsett!"

"Trader Loy!" Sorrel shouted as a startled, furious roar burst from the crowd on the dock. "We made it very clear to all sponsors that during this ceremony there was to be no mention—"

"It was Trader Mab who raised the subject," Loy interrupted. "And it seems she has taken it into her head to overturn the decision of the Trust Committee and hand the Rosalyn Apprenticeship to a young woman who is unfit in every way to hold such a responsible position."

"It is not for you to decide who is fit to be my Apprentice, Loy," snapped Mab. "The terms of the Rosalyn Trust clearly state that the Trader Rosalyn has the final word."

"The Trader Rosalyn when she is in her right mind!" barked Loy. "Not the Trader Rosalyn when she has just risen from her bed after being struck down by a murdering sorcerer who was the father of one of the finalists!"

There was an ominous rumbling from the dock.

Britta had begun to tremble. She felt dizzy and

sick. The lost memory that had been plaguing her for so long was tugging, tugging at her mind, but still it would not show itself.

"Trader Loy, you go too far!" cried Sorrel.

"I do not!" Loy retorted. "Everyone present must see that Mab is not herself! Leaving aside every other issue, the girl Britta entered the Rosalyn contest under false pretenses. She claimed to be an orphan, and to be related to Captain Gripp. Plainly she is neither."

"Britt didn't claim it!" Gripp roared. "*I* claimed it! An' Mab knew full well—"

"I knew that Captain Gripp thought a great deal of Britta," Mab broke in firmly, drowning him out. "And as for a few slight errors on the entry form—this is no time to abide by pettifogging rules! The point of the Rosalyn contest is to choose the best possible Apprentice. I have chosen Britta, and I have explained why. That should be enough."

"It is not enough," said Loy, meeting her glare with one of his own. "The Rosalyn Trust Committee cannot knowingly reward deceit without bringing dishonor to itself and its great history."

"Pompous poppycock!" Mab snorted, but clearly she was shaken. The strain was telling on her, Britta could see. Deep furrows had appeared between her brows. Her painted eyelids were drooping.

Sorrel regarded her thoughtfully, then seemed to come to a decision. He stepped forward, smoothing his moustache. His eyes were red, but he had wiped his face and looked almost his dapper self once more.

"I thank you, Trader Loy, for making your point with such calm and firmness," he said, smiling pleasantly at Loy and making one of his neat little bows. "You and your daughter both value calm and firmness very highly, I know, and I also know how much of Vashti's trading success is owed to … to those excellent qualities."

Loy blinked, and a tiny nerve jumped in his top lip. Beside him, Vashti became very still.

"Yes indeed," Sorrel went on smoothly. "I was reminded of it just this morning. While waiting for the *Star of Deltora* to dock, I began looking through all the finalists' files—to pass the time, you know. On this second glance, I was quite struck by the receipt for Vashti's test trade in Del. With one gold coin, Vashti secured a fine leather belt worth three! A remarkable bargain! Why, that receipt almost deserves to be put on public view, as a model of what calm and firmness can achieve!"

"Sorrel, if all this is supposed to convince me—" Mab began dangerously, but Loy, who had been whispering hurriedly with Vashti, spoke at the same moment.

"My daughter wishes me to withdraw my objection regarding the errors on Britta's entry form," he announced, his face like stone. "Vashti believes that while deceit is never right, it should be overlooked in this case."

"Ah," murmured Sorrel, as the other Committee members exclaimed in surprise. "How generous!"

"I cannot believe it!" Jewel muttered.

Neither could Britta. And Mab was looking thunderstruck. But Sky was grinning at Sorrel in frank admiration.

"It must have been something Sorrel said," Britta whispered to Jewel, her eyes on Sky's grin.

"But all Sorrel did was spout a lot of bilge about his wretched files and Vashti's calm and firmness!" Jewel hissed back.

Calm and firmness ... Suddenly Britta saw the light. She remembered the last line of Vashti's note to her parents on the night of the final test in Del—*I trust that calm and firmness will help me to succeed.* And she remembered later seeing Vashti walking confidently into the big leather goods store in Anchor Street—the store called "Calme and Furness."

"Calm and firmness—Calme and Furness!" she breathed. "It must be a joke in Vashti's family. She used it to send her father a message. He arranged for Calme and Furness to let her have a leather belt for a third of its true price! He must have secretly paid the difference! Sorrel realized it this morning, when he saw the receipt again and remembered the note. He was threatening to tell!"

Jewel shook her head in confusion. She had only heard half of what Britta had whispered, and she had not read Vashti's note. But Britta did not dare to say any more. Sorrel was stepping back, nodding slightly at Mab.

"Good," Mab said, still eyeing Loy and Vashti in amazement. "So, to continue … Britta of Del—"

The elegant woman beside Sorrel cleared her throat and held up her hand. Mab broke off with a scowl.

"I am sorry, Mab," the woman said earnestly. "It pains me to stand between you and the finalist you prefer, but my first duty is to protect the Rosalyn Trust, and I must speak."

"Yes, Trader Freck?" Sorrel said hurriedly, as Mab pressed her lips into a hard line.

The woman squared her shoulders. "There is still the matter of the trade. Trade is, and must be, at the heart of the Rosalyn contest, and in this case I do not accept that any real trade was made."

Finding their courage, the other members of the Trust Committee nodded. Even Sorrel was plainly finding it difficult to disagree.

"A real trade certainly *was* made," said Mab. "If you have heard the story, Trader Freck, you know that Britta traded for our lives on the Isle of Tier."

"I have heard enough to convince me that the trade was a sham," Freck persisted. "It was a trade in name only. The fact that the bargain was later broken might be overlooked. But a true trade means that each party gives something up. The finalist Britta gave up nothing. She merely had to kiss her father good-bye."

The crowd on the dock jeered and shouted in disgust. Britta swayed against Jewel. In the misty darkness of her mind a cracked voice echoed, filling her with pain.

I want to hear you call me "Father" once more ...

"Be silent!" Mab's voice cracked like a whip, cutting through the voice in Britta's mind, instantly quieting the crowd.

"That is better," Mab said more soberly, but still in tones loud enough for the people on the dock to hear. "Now, listen to me and listen well! For various reasons I had hoped to avoid this for the present, but I accept that Trader Freck has made a case that must be answered—if the dry letter of the law is all that counts."

She nodded to Freck, who bowed warily.

"First, forget everything you have heard or thought you knew," Mab said. "Now! Britta cannot tell you what she traded in the cavern of the Staff, because her memory of it has been blotted out. Hara, Kay, Sky, Jewel and Vashti cannot tell you, because they do not know it. But I can tell you—because at the time the trade was done, the King of Tier believed me to be safely dead."

She paused. Her bright crest of hair blazed, in bizarre contrast to her gaunt face. Her blue-painted eyelids and hooked nose made her look more than ever like an elderly parrot. But there was nothing absurd about her.

"In the cavern of the Staff, Britta made a bargain with the King of Tier," she said. "His part of the bargain was life and freedom for Britta and her companions. Her part was ... the thing she valued most in the world."

A ripple ran through the watching crowd. Britta heard Jewel grunt in confusion. Her own mind seemed to have gone blank.

"Our lives were in peril, and Britta plainly felt that she had no choice but to agree to the terms she was offered," Mab continued. "If she had been alone she might not have done so." She smiled faintly. "But then again, perhaps she might. Britta has a great zest for life. In that, she very much resembles her late father."

For the first time, she faltered, but after only a brief pause she lifted her chin and went on.

"The King of Tier asked that Britta call him 'Father' once more, give him her kiss, leave him without another word and then forget him and never speak his name again. It was a touching scene, in its way. The wraiths who worshipped the Staff certainly thought so."

She cocked her head. "I did not find it touching. For me it was— abominable! It chilled me to the bone, because I could see what no one else but Britta knew. The King of Tier was not Dare Larsett. He was Mikah, first captain of the *Star of Deltora*."

17 - Memory

Bellows of shock, disbelief and horror burst from hundreds of throats. The sound crashed over the deck like a mighty wave. Mab stood calmly waiting for it to pass, her eyes locked on Britta's face.

But Britta could not see Mab. She could not hear the roar of the crowd, or Gripp cursing at the top of his voice, or Sorrel gabbling questions.

She was remembering. With Mab's words, the blocked memory that had teased and nagged at her for weeks had burst into the open and flooded her mind.

At last she saw again the King of Tier on his golden throne. She saw Mikah, who had stolen her father's treasure, her father's life and her father's name. And she saw herself moving towards him, knowing that what she was about to do would confirm in the minds of the wraiths and everyone else present that he was the man he claimed to be.

How she had longed to cry out that he was a murdering impostor—that he was not her father, not Dare Larsett! But she had made her bargain. She could not break it. Even if she had been tempted to do so, the fiery spark deep in the King's hollow eyes had warned her that her life and the lives of her companions depended on her silence.

She had guessed who he was before, of course. She had begun to suspect it when she realized that only Mikah could have known that her father's name was hated in Del, because Mikah had written the note accusing him. She had been sure when the King made no response at all to the words her father had said to her so often.

The world is wide, and full of wonders ...

The raw memory was agonizing. Britta found herself sagging against Jewel, moaning with the pain of it. But then through the chaos that reigned in her mind she was recalling her second visit to the cavern.

She remembered whispering orders to the goozli, once she had realized why fate had brought them together. She remembered the King striking out at her. She remembered waking to find him dead, and the goozli in possession of the Staff, offering it to her and smiling as she refused it ...

Please do with it what Tier would have wished.

And she remembered stumbling after the goozli as it dragged the Staff through the thick of the silent forest to the shore. She remembered the little creature rolling the Staff down into the lapping, hissing water, the Staff dissolving into glittering sand, the wraiths caressing her and vanishing.

Then the turtles had departed, as if the sorcerer Tier himself had let them go—as if his spirit, too, was finally satisfied and at peace.

Slowly the pain ebbed and the real world came back into focus. Now Britta could hear Jewel muttering her name over and over again. Now she could see Captain Gripp limping towards her, leaning on the arm of Jewel's sponsor. She could see Sky, looking stunned. She could see Sorrel and Kay, both in tears. And she could see Mab, whose eyes were still fixed on hers.

"So now do you see what Britta traded for our lives?" Mab thundered. "Do you see what she was trading with that word, that kiss, that promise to forget? She was trading her chance to clear her father's name. She was trading her own future!"

"This cannot be!" Trader Freck cried wildly, as again the crowd roared. "Captain Mikah is buried in the harbor graveyard! His poor bones were lashed to the wheel of the drifting *Star of Deltora*—and the hook that he wore after he lost his hand to a sea serpent was with them! His final letter is framed, hanging on the wall in the Traders' Hall!"

"The bones buried in the graveyard, beneath a lying tombstone, are the bones of Dare Larsett," said Mab, her face as hard as iron. "Only his left hand is missing—the hand that held the Staff. Mikah took

Dare's hand for himself—and the Staff with it."

There were groans from the crowd. Freck winced and shuddered.

"He did it with a single slash of his cutlass, no doubt," Mab went on without flinching. "Then he used the magic of the Staff still clutched in the fingers to seal the hand to his own wrist. I saw it, Trader Freck—Dare Larsett's hand joined to Mikah's arm! I saw it with my own eyes!"

"Ah, the treacherous scum!" Gripp muttered, reaching Britta at last and patting her shoulder clumsily. "Ah, Britt—to think of it!" His face was wet with tears, and Britta knew that he was weeping for her father as much as for her.

"And as for Mikah's famous note," Mab went on remorselessly, "what he wrote was true, no doubt, except for the one great lie. Somehow Dare Larsett claimed the Staff—told it his name, and took it in his hand—that is certain. But every wicked thing Mikah accused Dare of doing afterward, he did himself. The viper even finished the note with a sneering message for me: 'I cannot say how bitterly I now regret leaving her service to sail with Dare Larsett.' Pah! Of course he could not say how much he regretted it! He did not regret it at all!"

Scowling, she waited for the tumult on the dock to subside. Only when complete silence had fallen did she speak again.

"But why the pretense? Safe on the Hungry Isle,

with the Staff of Tier at his command, why should Mikah care if everyone in the Silver Sea knew what he had done?"

Sorrel made a muffled sound, and Mab half smiled. "It seems that Trader Sorrel, at least, has guessed the answer to that. Well, Sorrel?"

"According to legend, the Staff of Tier bonded to the name and flesh of its Master, and would slay anyone else who tried to claim it," Sorrel said flatly. "Mikah had to make sure that neither the Staff nor the wraiths of the island ever learned that 'Larsett' was not his true name, and that the hand that held the Staff was not his own."

The crimson had faded from Sorrel's face, which suddenly looked far older than it had before. Britta met his eyes and a lump rose in her throat as she saw the anguished pity there.

Mab nodded. "So he wrote the note that everyone in the nine seas has believed till now. He wanted to be certain that even the humblest crew members of the poorest fishing boat attacked by the Hungry Isle would curse the name 'Larsett' as they died, and so strengthen the lie."

"Pure wickedness!" growled Erin of Broome, glancing at Britta.

"A cunning plan," Mab said calmly. "And for over eight years it worked, though I suspect that Mikah's control of the Staff was always less steady than its true Master's would have been. Then disaster struck.

Fate brought to Tier someone who could expose the impostor. Larsett's daughter—no longer the child she had been when Mikah last saw her on the newly built *Star of Deltora*, but a strong young woman who refused to be overcome by the shadows of her past."

A sighing murmur rippled through the crowd. Britta felt Captain Gripp's hand tighten on her shoulder. She heard Jewel mutter something, but did not catch the words.

Mab shrugged. "I would also recognize Mikah, of course, but he could strike *me* down, as in fact he did, without raising any suspicion. Britta was a different story. The wraiths knew who she was. How could Mikah kill, or even refuse to meet, a girl who was supposed to be his lost, beloved daughter?"

She smiled grimly. "So for once in his life, he behaved like a good trader. He turned what seemed to be a disaster into a golden opportunity. He decided to force Britta to pretend that he was who he claimed to be—her father, Larsett, the rightful Master of the Staff. The wraiths would never doubt him after that, whatever happened. He would be safe forever."

"That scoundrel was no trader worthy of the name!" Jewel burst out. "Once he had what he wanted he broke the bargain and tried to kill us all! If Britta had not somehow—"

She shut her mouth abruptly as Mab cast her a stony look.

"There is only one other matter I wish to raise

here," Mab said. "Some people—" here she gave the briefest of glances at Trader Loy "—may be tempted to say that while Britta's father may not have been the villain we thought he was, he was a villain all the same. Such people might say that Mikah and Larsett were two of a kind—both so greedy for the riches, power and eternal life that the Staff of Tier could give its Master that they fought over their prize to the death, and Larsett lost. Well, I am going to leave it to Dare himself to answer that charge."

She jerked her head at Healer Kay, who handed her a small black book.

Mab held the book high. "This is Dare Larsett's private journal of his last voyage. I found it earlier today, tucked with a few other items in a hidden safe in the Chief Trader's cabin. I did not know the safe existed. I only discovered it this morning because its door flap had fallen open—a jolt when we docked, perhaps ..."

Or a goozli slipping out and leaving the flap open behind it so there would be no sound, Britta thought, pressing her hand to her skirt pocket. Beside her, Captain Gripp was muttering excitedly, exclaiming that he had forgotten all about the safe, but she was only dimly aware of him. Her whole attention was focused on the book in Mab's hand.

"I have read it," Mab was saying. "Much of it is personal, and of no concern to anyone except Dare's family and close friends. But I want to share with you one particular passage, very near to the beginning."

Taking her time, she opened the book and found the place she wanted. As she began to read, her mellow voice ringing out over the ship and the crowded dock beyond, Britta could almost see the hasty, confident writing on the open page.

<u>1 day out from Two Moons:</u> My Two Moons trade was successful, so an hour ago I told Captain Mikah the real purpose of our voyage. As I expected, Mikah was excited & proud, asked no awkward questions & showed not a trace of fear. Mikah is a brave man with very little imagination & a great desire for fame. This is why I chose him, of course, but I am glad my instincts did not lead me astray.

It was a great relief to share the secret I have kept for so long. Ever since I found Bar-Enoch's final resting place two years ago I have known that complete secrecy was vital. I longed to confide in those I loved, but I did not dare. If word of my quest leaked out, the Star of Deltora would be watched intently, & my chances of taking the Staff from under the noses of the Collectors of Illica would be nil. Not to mention that I may fail, or die in the attempt!

Mostly I refuse to think of that, but I would be a fool to deny that the risks are very great. There have been times, I confess, when I have been tempted to forget the whole, mad scheme. Then I think of Sheevers & all the other sad, damaged souls that the Staff of Tier could make whole again, & I know I must go on.

I only have to find the strength to fight the lure of the Staff for as long as it takes to sail home from Illica.

I only have to be its Master till I can carry it to the palace of Del, where it can be passed safely on to our king by the same means that (I hope) it will pass from Bar-Enoch to me. With Deltora's king, the Staff of Tier will be safe. The magic at his command will protect him from its corrupting power. In his hand, the Staff will cure, not harm. It will be a blessing instead of a curse.

I feel that my whole life has shaped me for this task. At last there is something I can do for my people and my land, some return I can make for what they have given me.

Mab looked up, marking her place with one finger. Her audience was utterly still. Captain Gripp's hand was shaking on Britta's shoulder. Many people were weeping.

Mab, too, had tears in her eyes. "That is the heart of it," she said. "But for those who knew Dare well, I had better read the rest." She smiled slightly, and looked down at the book again.

Ah ... how noble that sounds! I can almost hear Mab laughing at me.

"Are you pretending that you are being purely selfless,

Dare Larsett?" my old friend would jeer, if she read this. "Are you pretending that the very thought of capturing the lost Staff that has fascinated you since you were a boy does not send your cursed treasure hunter's blood racing?"

No, I will not pretend that, Mab. I am doing this for Sheevers & all who still suffer from the horrors of the Shadowlands invasion, certainly. But I am doing it for myself as well. The thrill of the chase is bubbling in my veins. At this moment, I feel more alive than I have ever done in my life.

Mab tightened her lips and closed the book. "So there you have it," she said simply. "Dare Larsett was neither villain nor saint. He was a clever, conceited, reckless, loving, generous rascal—and a great trader, who all of us can be proud to have known."

She drew herself up, ruthlessly forcing Sky and Kay to bear her full weight. "The Apprentice ceremony will now continue. Britta of Del, daughter of Maarie and Larsett, please step forward!"

18 - Friends

Mab had her way for the next half hour, but the moment the solemn ceremony was over, Healer Kay took command. As frenzied applause and cheers rang out over the harbor, Britta was whisked away from the flock of chattering well-wishers surging towards her, and taken below.

There, in the blessed peace of the traders' dining room, she was able to collect her scattered thoughts. She was able to come to terms with her recovered memories of the Hungry Isle and decide which ones she could safely share. She was able to read a little of her father's diary. After a time, Jewel and Sky were allowed to join her, for Kay was shrewd enough to know that their company would do her patient good, not harm.

While the beaming Davvie ran in and out bringing hot tea and a basket of fresh fruit, soft cheese and crusty rolls from shore, the three friends talked little, and then only of small things. Jewel and Sky asked no questions about the two little pottery lanterns, the delicate silver brooch and the small black book ranged on the table in front of Britta. They knew she would talk about the contents of the secret safe when she was ready.

"If Sorrel knew that Vashti had cheated in Del, I cannot understand why he was still going to let her win!" Jewel complained.

Sky shrugged. "He felt he had no other choice, I daresay. Then Mab rose from what was supposed to be her deathbed, and everything changed. *Then* Sorrel could make his veiled threat to expose Vashti's little game and force Loy to back down."

"Sorrel should not have just threatened!" Jewel fumed, snatching up a sweetplum and biting into it as savagely as if it were Trader Loy himself. "It makes me wild to think that Vashti has walked off this ship with people believing she is generous when she is quite the opposite—and dishonest in the bargain!"

"Vashti lost," Sky pointed out calmly. "The cheating gained her nothing. And as things are, public scandal has been avoided and the dignity of the Rosalyn Trust has been preserved. Those things mean a lot to old Sorrel, you know."

Jewel snorted. Plainly she was not convinced.

"The sad thing is," Britta found herself saying, "that Vashti could no doubt be a very good trader if only her father would trust in her talent and leave her alone."

"There is such a thing as being too softhearted, Britta," Jewel said severely. "What has gotten into you?"

"I daresay she has been taking lessons from Mab," Sky said with a straight face. "Why, just last night we had yet another example of Mab's tender heart!"

It was a blessing to laugh, and laugh they did, very heartily. By now they had all realized that Mab's refusal to see anyone the night before had been simply a matter of vanity. Mab's hair had grown during her illness, and she had been determined to stay hidden until the red dye Kay had applied to the white roots had done its work. She had not cared a jot for anyone else's suffering.

"Still, the dye must surely have dried by this morning," Jewel said, wiping her streaming eyes with the back of her hand. "Why did the old rogue not show herself as soon as we landed?"

"She was reading this," Britta said quietly, touching the small book in front of her.

She felt the mood in the room grow tense. She knew that her friends were both longing to know more of what the diary said. They would not press her, but she was very aware that this precious, private time with them would soon be ending.

Very soon, Traders Sorrel and Freck would reach the little shop in the city's center. They would break the day's astounding news to Britta's mother and sister. Then, almost certainly, they would bring Maarie and Margareth to the harbor. And after that, it would be some time before Britta would see Jewel and Sky alone again.

So, though her feelings were still very tender, Britta opened the book and turned to the page she wanted. "I have not had time to read it all," she murmured. "I have only glanced through it. But this part—right at the end—I want you to hear."

Her voice a little unsteady, she began to read:

> 1 hour out from Illica: The deed is done. The Staff passed from Bar-Enoch's hand to mine as safely as I hoped. I am sure that Bar-Enoch took it from the turtle man Tier's body in the same way. Bar-Enoch is known to have spent time with the turtle people of Two Moons. Then, of course, there are those tales about him "talking to himself" in his cabin ...

"So your father learned something in Two Moons that helped him break the curse," Sky whispered eagerly, as Britta stopped for breath. "Some sort of chant or spell, perhaps! Does he say what it was?"

Britta shook her head. Even in his private journal, Dare Larsett had not revealed the secret of the goozli she was sure he had carried out of the Two Moons swamplands to help him secure the Staff of Tier.

She stared into space for a moment, wondering about that goozli. What had happened to it when her father died at Mikah's hands? Then, suddenly, she knew. She remembered her own goozli shaking its head when she begged it to help her friends if she was killed. The goozli knew more than she did about the magic that bonded them. It knew that if Britta died, its own life would end.

So Dare Larsett's goozli had returned to the clay of which it was made. Its dust had mingled with Larsett's blood in the *Star's* cargo hold. Just as the far older dust of Bar-Enoch's goozli had no doubt mingled with the sand of the death chamber in Illica.

"Britta?"

Jewel's anxious voice recalled Britta to herself. She looked back down at the diary, and read on.

Thank the stars, I managed to keep my head. I told the Staff my name & held it for the shortest possible time before thrusting it into the lead-lined box. But still, what I felt while it was in my hand was ... intense. Dangerous.

Mikah came in from the cavern mouth where I had made him wait, and together we got the box back to the ship. Now it is chained securely in the cargo hold and the Star is underway once more.

It was a good night's work, but for one thing. I have lost the odi shell hair clip I had bought for Maarie. I took it from the safe & carried it with me, thinking it would bring me luck, & now I cannot find it. It must have fallen from my pocket in that cursed cavern. I hate to think of it lying there in the foul darkness. I hope its loss is not a bad omen ...

Jewel and Sky had both gasped at the mention of the hair clip, but Britta did not look up. She took a breath to steady herself, turned the page and went on reading.

1 day out from Illica: The Staff nags at me from its place in the cargo hold, but I grit my teeth and try to busy myself with other things. My main problem at present is Mikah, whose maimed arm has begun paining him terribly, poor fellow. He says he hurt it while we were moving the Staff to the ship, though he said nothing at the time ...

2 days out from Illica: Healer Vine is baffled as to the cause of Mikah's trouble & the usual remedies seem to have no effect. The pain must be truly agonizing, because Mikah has even left off wearing the hook that serves him as a left hand, saying that he cannot bear to strap it on.

He keeps pleading with me to go with him to the hold & use the Staff to help him. I have refused so far, but I confess that the thought of feeling the Staff's power again is very tempting—and, after all, it would be in a good cause ...

3 days out from Illica: Today Mikah begged me on his knees to ease his suffering, and I agreed. Why not? Mikah needs help and surely I have the right to experience—just once—what it means to be Master of the Staff that cures all ills! We will go to the hold tonight.

Britta closed the book. There was no more to read. The rest of the pages were blank.

"So that was how Mikah did it," she heard Jewel hiss. "Ah, the cunning, lying villain!"

"The lure of the Staff overpowered him," said Sky in a flat voice. "He did not have the strength to resist it."

Looking up, Britta met his troubled eyes and knew that he was thinking of his own longing for the Staff.

"Even Father's will was weakening by the end, despite all his planning," she murmured. "You can see by what he wrote how badly he wanted to feel the power of the Staff again."

"Perhaps!" barked a voice from the doorway. "But unlike Mikah he would not have killed for it."

Startled, the friends jumped to their feet as Mab hobbled in, forcing Kay to stumble along with her or let her fall.

'Mikah was always jealous of Dare—ever since they were boys," Mab said. "He was wild to be a trader, you know. I told him he did not have it in him to be a good one, and I was right. He knew nothing of people."

She snorted. "If he had, he would still be alive today, because he would not have broken his bargain on the island. He would not have felt he needed to. He would have known that Britta's honor as a trader would have forced her to keep her part of the bargain till her life's end. Is that not so, Britta?"

Britta nodded and bowed her head.

"Very well, Kay!" Mab snapped, as Kay tugged at her arm. "By all the little fishes, girl, I have the whole day to lie on my bunk! But I am nearly done here. Britta, this was just found under the deck planks of the landing boat. Kay tells me it is yours."

She plumped something into Britta's hand. It was the odi shell hair clip.

"I will not ask how you came by it," Mab said, darting a suspicious look at Sky. "But from what I read in your father's diary, it is treasure trove, so nothing to do with the Rosalyn Trust."

"Thank you, Mab," Britta managed to say.

"You might also like to know that I had a few words with Vorn and Collin of Illica just now," Mab went on. "As I suspected, the young fools had no idea in the world how much gold their sunrise pearl would bring. I have promised to sell it for them at the best possible price, and in return they have agreed to give you half of the proceeds."

She scowled as Britta began faltering a confused protest. "Curse you, girl, stiffen your spine! The money is owed to you! Your family needs it! And Collin and Vorn will have enough gold left to build ten boatyards, if they wish."

At last she let Kay drag her to the door, but in the doorway she dug in her heels and turned back.

"Oh, just one more thing," she said carelessly.

"Jewel and Sky, it seems that while I am by no means cured, I am not to die quite yet. So I have decided that if you are willing you might join Britta and me on the *Star of Deltora*'s next few trading voyages. If I cannot be young myself, I can at least surround myself with the young. Besides, you need experience and Del trading needs some new blood."

Her lips twitched as Jewel punched the air, hooting with delight, and Sky stammered his amazed thanks.

"But there is to be no more willful damage to property, Jewel of Broome!" she warned, shaking her bony finger. "And as for you, Sky of Rithmere—no more treasure hunting!"

With that, Mab took her leave. Britta, whose cup of joy was now overflowing, wondered if she had noticed that while Jewel had rashly sworn to be a model of caution in the future, Sky had only smiled.

19 - And Then?

A week later, Britta sat in the little shelter at the end of the harbor graveyard with Jantsy by her side. Behind her, waves lapped gently against the seawall. Her heart was very full. The king and queen of Deltora had attended the ceremony to honor Dare Larsett, but now they had gone. The crowds who had come to witness the great event had gradually faded away as well.

Now, as the day ebbed, only a few people still lingered among the gravestones. Britta's eyes drifted lazily from one group to another.

There were Jewel and Sky, talking with Collin and Vorn, Erin of Broome and Captain Hara. Now and then Sky glanced in Britta's direction as if he wished she would join them, but for the moment she was content to stay where she was.

There was Mab, with Healer Kay and Captain

Gripp, moving slowly towards the Traders' Hall. Bosun the polypan was dancing around them, madly chewing a toffee that Kay had found for him.

There was Trader Sorrel, standing in the shadows with Lean Alice and Master Sheevers, who clutched to his chest the two lanterns that his great friend Larsett had found for him in Maris. Sheevers was calmer now, and Britta knew why. She herself had heard the king tell the old potter gently that he did not have to fear—if he wished to remain in his den and seek lanterns, then in his den he could stay. But from now on food and clothing would be brought to him from the palace—a gift, the king had said, from Dare Larsett.

And finally Britta's eyes rested on the last, and nearest, group.

Her mother, the odi shell clip shining in her hair, a new, sad peace shining in her worn but still beautiful face, was standing by the fresh stone that marked Larsett's grave. Close beside Maarie was Margareth, her hand pressed to the flower-shaped silver brooch pinned to the collar of her shirt.

Words from her father's diary swam before Britta's eyes. Larsett had found gifts for his family, as well as for Sheevers, in Maris.

... for my dear Maarie, who puts up with me despite my faults, an odi shell hair clip that says what is in my heart. For my gentle Margareth, a silver brooch that is almost as pretty as she is herself. For Britta, my restless little bird, a length of silk in all the colors of the rainbow—including soffa blue, which is becoming very rare.

Maarie, of course, will say that such colors are not proper for a young lady of Del. Perhaps they are not, but they could not be better for a trader of the kind that Britta wants to be. I will keep the silk on a shelf where I can see it, I think. It pleases my eye as much as I think it will please Britta's.

I hope that whenever she looks at it, she will remember that there will be a time when she can wear it—when she is grown, and we are sailing the wide seas together in the Star of Deltora.

Hot tears sprang into Britta's eyes and rolled down her cheeks.

She felt Jantsy stir and put his arm around her. She wanted to tell him that she did not need comfort—not really—but she could not speak, and after a moment she realized that she did not need to say a word. Jantsy understood. So she just leaned into his shoulder and let the tears fall, feeling the bitterness and mourning of the last eight years draining from her heart. And Jantsy simply waited, while slowly the light faded from the graveyard, and the people standing among the graves became little more than shadows.

Even when the tears ended at last, and Britta pulled a little away from him to sit upright, Jantsy said nothing, but kept his soothing silence. Britta sniffled, and with a watery smile pulled her handkerchief from the pocket of the straight blue skirt she had put on for her mother's peace of mind.

"So much has changed, Jantsy," she found herself saying.

"But some things have not, and never will," he said. "Like the stars in the sky, some things are forever."

Impulsively she put out her hand to him, but at that moment the harbor clock began to strike seven and her mother called her name in an anxious voice that could not be ignored. With a sigh Britta stood up, pushing the loose hairpins back into the knot at the nape of her neck, tucking her shirt more firmly into the waistband of her skirt.

She thought of the soft silk blouse and the scarlet skirt still hanging in the *Star*, and just for an instant the old trapped feeling stabbed at her again.

"There, you see?" Jantsy said lightly, standing up with her. "Some things never change. Mothers, for example." She saw his teeth flash white as he grinned.

Maarie and Margareth were already hurrying after the others to the Traders' Hall. The reception that had been planned was to begin at seven, and it would not be polite to be late. Food and drink would be waiting.

And more speeches, no doubt, Britta thought, smothering a sigh.

At her father's grave, she stopped. The air was

heavy with the scent of the flowers that lay heaped on the mound below the newly carved stone.

The world is wide, Britta, and full of wonders …

"I am glad Father's name will be remembered," she said. "But he is not here, Jantsy. His spirit is out there."

She turned back to the dark harbor that opened its arms to the wide, open sea. She saw the lights of the *Star of Deltora*, rocking gently at anchor.

And suddenly she was filled with piercing joy.

For now there would be speeches and chatter. Then, for a time, there would be the safe, familiar comforts of home. She would say good night to Margareth in their tiny bedroom above the shop. She would help her mother choose new clothes and furniture. She would face the neighbors who flocked in, filled with goodwill, wanting to share in her family's joy. She would sit in the bakery, watching Jantsy work in the early morning, and walk with him in the cool of the evening.

But soon, very soon, she would return to the harbor.

And when she did, the *Star of Deltora* would be waiting.